PRAISE FC

The Girl in the White Cape

"*The Girl in the White Cape* immediately pulls you into a thrilling fairy tale world. Sapienza is a master world-builder. There's a smoothness, a wonderful control, to Sapienza's prose that allows us to gladly suspend our disbelief and excitedly immerse ourselves into the text. There isn't a sentence out of place in this book. I am in awe of it."

— JANINE NOEL, cofounder of Diablo Writers' Workshop

"*The Girl in the White Cape* is mesmerizing, creating parallel worlds, each holding reality and magic. The intertwining of reality and miracle takes form through Frank, Al, Elena, and others who propel this mesmerizing saga as evil is vanquished and virtue celebrated."

— JOAN MINNINGER, PHD, coauthor of *The Father Daughter Dance*, *Total Recall*, and *Free Yourself to Write*

"Gifted storyteller Barbara Sapienza awakens our childlike wonder as she invites us to explore the power of the feminine, of mystical knowing, and of trusting our heart in this beautifully crafted fairy tale of love and healing. Her rich characters, like a fine cabernet, made me want to savor each page."

— DONNA STONEHAM, author of *Catch Me When I Fall* and *The Thriver's Edge*

"I'll never go back to Golden Gate Park without thinking of white-caped Elena filling her bag with acorns under the oaks. Sapienza has conjured magic in the fairy-tale city of San Francisco, where a hero might be driving a cab and a witch may live next door."
—ANN LUDWIG, travel writer for *The New York Times*

"Though set in contemporary San Francisco, Barbara Sapienza's spellbinding *The Girl in the White Cape* invites you into an old-world fairy tale. Nearly fifteen-year-old Elena lives in a world apart. She longs to have 'normal' friends her age, but how can she escape alienation? How can anyone? Sapienza shows the way."
—DIANNE ROMAIN, author of *The Trumpet Lesson*

"I identify with Elena's journey as she faces the unknown and opens herself to magical connections with others. She is afraid, but she still leans into and trusts an inner intuition that guides her, teaching us that even as we encounter darkness, new ways of seeing can be found."
—GAIL WARNER, author of *Weaving Myself Awake: Voicing the Sacred Through Poetry*

"Author Barbara Sapienza has given us a gift of beauty and magic, one that spins us in a dizzying Russian fairy-tale land and then seamlessly back into modern-day San Francisco. She surprises and delights with the twists and turns of the book so that the reader is swept along into enjoyable and unexpected directions. Mythical and archetypal, *The Girl in the White Cape* is spellbinding!"
—CHERYL KRAUTER, author of *Odyssey of Ashes*

The Girl in
the White Cape

The Girl in the White Cape

A Novel

BARBARA SAPIENZA

SHE WRITES PRESS

Published 2023
Printed in the United States of America
Print ISBN: 978-1-64742-503-6
E-ISBN: 978-1-64742-504-3
Library of Congress Control Number: 2023900297

For information, address:
She Writes Press
1569 Solano Ave #546
Berkeley, CA 94707

Interior Design by Tabitha Lahr

She Writes Press is a division of SparkPoint Studio, LLC.

For my granddaughters,

Milla Sapienza
and
Isabella Farfan

Yet mystery and reality
Emerge from the same source.
This source is called darkness.

Darkness born from darkness.
The beginning of all understanding.

—LAO TZU, *Tao Te Ching*, Chapter 1

CHAPTER 1: The Doll

Elena, on the eve of her fifteenth birthday, closes the book of fairy tales and wonders what this year will bring. Resting in the attic room of the Russian church Our Lady of Sorrow, her head touches the book—a remnant from her childhood. The frayed pages of the fairy tales give off the scent of loneliness for all these years gone by without a mother.

She remembers how Father Al would read this book to her whenever she could not stop crying. Her favorite story, the one she insisted he read over and over, was "Vasilisa the Beautiful and Baba Yaga." She especially liked the part with the doll because she, too, had a doll she kept in her pocket. Even now, as she's about to turn fifteen, she keeps Kukla there. When she caresses her, she can hear Father Al whispering his kind words.

"Listen—hush, little child—listen for the unbroken cord," he would repeat until she stopped crying and peeped out from under the wool blanket.

His eyes, wet too, would drip tears over a smiling face. "Hug your little doll when you're sad and scared, ask her to help you. You know she's a gift from your mom."

Thus comforted, she would fall asleep with the little doll in her hand. In her dreams, she would see her beautiful mother standing in a garden, holding out the doll.

As the years passed, she sometimes wondered if she should ask Father Al what had happened to her mother, but thinking of asking always gave her a crick in her neck or a cramp in her stomach. She knew her mother would not have left her if not for a good reason. And besides, she didn't want to know what made that stiffness inside her. Still, each time Father got near the end of "Vasilisa the Beautiful" she would say, "Again, Father," hoping for some clue to the mystery. Again and again he read the story until she fell asleep—but no clues ever surfaced.

Though she knows the story by heart, she doesn't know its ending or what lies ahead for her. All she knows is she wakes up each morning in a cozy attic room with her lovely little Kukla tucked close into her side, and a sense of living in a dream—of being a storybook girl who goes every day, except Sundays, to Baba Vera and Dedushka Victor's.

As a child, Elena became Vasilisa the Beautiful. And like Vasilisa, she was adopted. Father Al found her on the doorstep of the church when she was just a few days old. Pinned to her infant nightie was a loving note from her mother, and in her bassinette was the beloved doll who has been her friend and confidante all these years since. Like Vasilisa, Elena keeps her doll in her pocket and goes into the woods to her baba's house, where magical things happen. Elena's baba is not Baba Yaga, however, but Baba Vera. Father Al says *baba* means grandma, but Elena doesn't think she's a real grandma like the old ladies who come to Father Al's masses and show him pictures of infants.

Elena doesn't think it's a coincidence that she grew up listening to this fairy tale. She wonders if Father Al has ever noticed the similarities between her and Vasilisa, or knows that Vasilisa was her imaginary friend for many years—one who made magic things happen, like a flying broom she could spin on to make herself dizzy; who helped her not to be afraid in the woods; who climbed with her up the low horizontal trunk of that old bay laurel in the courtyard all the way to where the trunk split, then swung down with her on the same branch to the garden floor, where they laughed themselves silly. She and her imaginary friend were sisters. *We imagined getting lost and found in the woods, we were best friends, and together, we were not so alone*, she remembers.

V used to say, "Make yourself dizzy, Elena—spin, spin. Don't be afraid." They knocked themselves out spinning, laughing, and falling down. Now Elena makes room for the mysterious nature of her life—like Kukla, who helps her to complete her tasks, and like Baba, who seems to have no age. Father Al says she's ageless.

Sometimes Elena imagines the fairy tale foreshadows her life. It's like having a map. Knowing that comforts her. She just has to stay within the borders and spin sometimes, like V told her to do long ago.

Elena rolls over and curls into the soft bed, clutching Kukla, contemplating the parts of the story that have holes in them. She's never understood, for instance, why Vasilisa got kicked out of her stepmother's house and was sent into the woods alone to find fire and then had to bring it back in a skull. Imagine! That's too weird! But then she's also never understood why Father Al started taking her every day to Baba Vera's house to work when she was just a little girl, when she would have been happy enough sorting prayer cards and playing with the rosaries in the church chapel or digging or swinging with her imaginary friend in the courtyard.

Baba Vera acts a bit like a witch. Elena's scared of her but Father Al says she shouldn't worry, "She took care of me and she's there like a grandmother to help you out." She knows he's telling her the truth by the way he looks into her eyes, the way his lips curve in a crescent moon, and the way his long, smooth hands pat her shiny red hair. Sometimes he takes her hand in his as a reassurance. And yet Baba can scare the heck out of her.

One day when they were walking across Golden Gate Park, Elena asked Father Al who Baba really was and why she couldn't just stay in the pretty church with him with the colorful candles reflecting on Saint Seraphin, her favorite saint. He said that Baba, who he sometimes called Auntie, had helped him when Elena came to stay at his church—even advised him. Then, walking with a lighter step, he said, "Baba is the eternal spring; she just keeps flowing."

In that moment Elena's eyes must have lit up like a Christmas tree, because what he said about an eternal spring made her feel all wired inside with sparks. She loved water and the way it moved; she tried to fit Baba into that image.

Father Al chuckled. "That one! She never gets old."

Elena wanted to hear more about Father Al's experiences when he was a boy and more about Baba, the flowing stream, but she didn't ask. She was content just to stay with his light step. She was learning that each thing had its time and place and maybe this was one of those places to hold back. Like Vasilisa, Elena shouldn't ask *certain* questions, and this was a certain question.

The holes in the fairy tale seemed to mirror the holes in her life. Sometimes things seem strange—but maybe that's the magic.

Kukla rests close to Elena's chest, bestowing body warmth as if her red pinafore and red shoes send out the fire of the sun. Under her little white crown lay the silkiest ringlets of blond hair, about an inch long. Elena wraps them around her finger and, hugging Kukla's chest, Elena repeats the words of the letter left to her by her birth mother all those years ago, words she knows by heart:

I leave you this little doll with my blessing. Keep it with you always and do not show it to a soul. If you are ever in trouble, give the doll something to eat and ask its advice. It will take your food and tell you what to do.

In the morning, the soft light of dawn flows through Elena's dormer window. As an infant she slept downstairs in a crib near Father Al's chapel, listening to his Kyrie lullabies, until she got to an age when stories became more interesting to her and she began requesting "Vasilisa the Beautiful."

The book peeks from under the pillow, reminding her that she read it last night, poring over each colorful page. She smiles and rolls over—feeling the new day, remembering it's the start of her sixteenth year. Today something shines inside, like the sunrise, yet there is struggle. It's as if she's been climbing a mountain and she's about to get to the top—but then what? These feelings seem contradictory and she's not sure how to hold them both side by side. She gets a cramp in her stomach when she thinks of the lady who pinned the soft doll to her nightie long ago.

Kukla is nested in beside her, warming her. Kukla's soft, not a lacquered nesting doll like the ones she's seen in a Russian store on Geary Boulevard. Elena prefers to think that Kukla has a long thread of sister dolls—others like her who wear special crowns, red pinafores, and satin shoes. What if a whole family exists? Sometimes she envisions a long shiny braid of hair connecting Kukla to dolls in front of her with others that will come following behind. It's like every little girl has or will have her own little doll to help her—like they are all connected in a silky tapestry of time. That thought gives her pause.

She hugs her doll. *Thank you for being here with me. You help and protect me. Because of you I can do all those silly tasks Baba Vera gives me.*

Elena does the planting and gardening, harvesting and canning, sorting and pairing the good from the bad, cooking and cleaning, and now carving Baba's favorite cuts of meat, like tenders and flanks. The amount of work Baba gives is demanding, and Elena doesn't know how she completes it, other than for Kukla giving her the strength to do so. She knows she must stay focused. Baba is strict and more than that. Father Al calls her a taskmaster. "She's testing you because she knows you can do it," he tells Elena, then adds, "She wants to see you succeed."

Sometimes, though, it feels like she's trying to trick her. Oftentimes, Elena doesn't believe she's got her back after all.

Father Al used to say Baba came from heaven. But mostly, Elena senses Baba is at the beginning of that line of dolls she imagines, leading the way. Baba lives her life like a dream, with all its nonsense parts running wild, and when the dream work is done, the images dissolve and fly away.

After dressing, Elena takes her white cape and red bag and leaves Our Lady, heading under the blue dome through the foyer. Father doesn't greet her with her usual Russian sweet bread and tea. He must be with a parishioner.

As she passes through the vestibule, she hears a woman shrieking. She covers her ears, shielding herself from the shrill voice, and exits quickly out the main entrance and onto the street. Outside, she sees a young man parked in his taxi in front of the church, waiting. *For whom?* she wonders. *Is he waiting for the screaming woman?* Odd—she's never seen a cab parked in front of Our Lady. Most people walk to the church.

There's no one else on the street; the houses in the neighborhood quietly shine in the morning autumn sun. The taxi driver's head stays down when Elena slips around the yellow cab and takes a peek inside. A long ponytail runs down his back, and his head is tilted forward, heavy-lidded eyes staring at a point below his steering wheel. She thinks he might be napping, until she glimpses a cell phone in his lap.

She's not allowed to have a cell phone, and Father Al doesn't even have one, so she doesn't know much about how they work. All she knows is that people walk past her on the street with their eyes glued to the small screen, never noticing her as she passes them. She's aware how easy it is for her to glide through space unnoticed, like a sleek cat, in this world where people seem to pay so little attention—like this man who has not even noticed her presence. She sometimes imagines she's invisible—and she might believe it, too, if kids didn't ruin it by staring at her sometimes.

The first time she noticed other kids staring at her she was eight, walking from Our Lady across Golden Gate Park with Father Al. The kids were coming from the opposite direction, crossing the park.

"Who are they, Father? And why are their clothes so different from mine?" asked eight-year-old Elena. She looked at her white woolen cape and black skirt, fingered the red bandana on her head.

The boys wore colorful pants and sporty jackets with names and numbers on them; the girls wore print dresses and skirts, tight-legged stockings, and bright-colored jackets with zippers. They all carried backpacks with names like Jansport and The North Face on them and they chatted loudly, playing and pulling at each other as they approached . . . until they noticed her. That's when they stared.

When they stared, she stared back.

"These children are walking to school," Father Al explained.

"School?"

"Yes, they go every day to learn things like you do."

"But I don't see them at Baba's." She wondered if they were under some spell—if they were working alongside her but she couldn't see them. Elena, steeped in magic, couldn't fathom that there might be another school they went to where she didn't go.

"They go to public school," Father Al said.

"Do they have a Baba Yaga too?"

"They do, though it's a woman or a man they call teacher."

"Is Baba Vera my teacher?"

"Yes."

"Why don't those children come to my school?" She pulled on his cassock. "Why don't I go to their school, Father?"

"Because you are special. You are not like them." His brow furrowed when he said this. "You are meant to study with Baba until she fulfills her plan."

"I don't understand."

"All you need to know for now is that she will keep you safe."

Though she trusted Father Al, she could see by the look on the children's faces that they found her mysterious, or at least different from them. Like the ducks, they traveled in a gaggle, while she walked with only a priest by her side. Momentarily she had that prickly feeling inside, like she got when she thought of her mother in the garden, holding up Kukla. Then she wondered briefly if any of the kids had a priest, or a doll—but whom could she ask?

Elena looked up at Father Al. His face was more serious than she wanted it to be.

"And I must keep you safe, too," he said. "When I was a child, I had a difficult time, and it was only Baba Vera's ways that kept me on course. Like you, I went to her house every day, and it was she who noticed my calling and steered me to become a priest."

Elena couldn't imagine Father Al as a child. And she knew nothing about children. The only ones she'd ever seen were those she passed in the park. She'd never spoken to any. She'd never had a friend her own age, except for V, and she was imaginary. Elena wished she had a friend like the children on the path—to be one of them and not be so different. Sometimes she felt like a lost girl; if it weren't for her doll, she'd be alone. She reached into her pocket and squeezed Kukla, who assured her someday she would have a friend.

So every weekday after the mass, when the sun was up, she and Father Al walked hand in hand across the park to Baba's cabin. On the way they often lingered at the ponds and trees to watch the bison and ducks who lived in Golden Gate Park.

Elena loved to walk beside Father Al, who always wore a black cassock and a funny hat. She loved how he walked at her pace. They were always in step. When she stopped to examine an autumn leaf or even a small mole scurrying underfoot, Father Al was looking at it too. She marveled at their *instepness*. It was as if they were one.

She remembers the day she told him she didn't want to go to Baba's house.

"Father, I don't want to go there today," she said one day.

"You don't have to go," he said. "Let's just walk into the park toward Middle Drive and then you can decide."

They crossed the park at 36th Avenue and walked west toward the bison field. It was cold outside, and the bison were huddling together in a family group like the ducks often did. Elena and Father Al stopped to watch.

"Look, they're wearing thick coats. How do they do it? Do they have a doll, Father?"

His eyebrows seemed to smile but he didn't laugh at her question. "Yes," he said. "I imagine they do."

By the time they crossed JFK and arrived at the duck pond on Middle Drive, she was content to continue on to the cabin alone, where her work would be set out for her.

Elena continues through the park toward Baba's. She loves how, now that she's a teenager, she can walk alone through this glorious park, so beautiful in all seasons. It's almost as if Father Al is right beside her.

As she reaches the duck pond, the wind picks up. She hastens her step. It's November and the leaves are changing to brown, yet one yellow leaf blows away from its branch, seeming to saunter above her head before landing in the moist earth. The trees, both deciduous and coniferous, drop cones or pine needles and colored leaves, making a rich mulch for the small insects that happily roam in the mix. She hears a raptor squeal off in the distance as smaller birds peep. Squirrels jockey about the trunks and branches. When she reaches the small pond, she sits and watches the ducks waking up, waddling from their evening rest. She counts them. Satisfied they are all there, she walks on out of the park.

Baba's house, a hidden cabin-style construction, sits behind a shop front on a busy street. This is where Victor, when he's home, builds wooden chairs, constructs bows and arrows, and makes brooms out of straw and herbs.

Elena crosses the street in front of their house and wonders what Baba Vera might make her do today. It seems she's graduated from dusting the skulls that hang on Baba's walls, or sweeping and piling hay into tall piles, to cutting meats into tenders and flanks. Most likely Baba Vera will continue teaching her about meat today. It seems like she is preparing Elena for food service and not the priesthood. Then again, she's never seen a girl priest.

Years ago, Baba shrieked, scaring the hell out of her, "The broomstick! You know what it's for, little girl? You remember?"

She laughed then, a hearty laugh—*like a madwoman.* She had no idea what she was talking about, but she recalled the tale where Baba Yaga flies in a mortar and pestle.

"Yeah, sure, you'll use that broom to fly over the neighborhood with your bow and arrow, looking for meat," Victor teased, meeting Elena's wide-eyed stare, making her feel more at ease.

Elena had never seen her fly, but if anyone could, it was Baba Vera.

When Elena enters the side passageway of the house, a dizzying feeling greets her, as though she's just stepped up on a merry-go-round like the one in Golden Gate Park. Is this spinning round and round part of that birthday feeling and the deep change she feels coming, or just the usual vertigo she gets near the cottage? She breathes deeply and walks toward the wooden gate that leads to the back of the house.

Bones and skulls line the side fence to the back entrance, none of them visible from the outside storefront on Taraval Street. Even though she's been coming here for seven years, it's still an electrifying experience to pass through these gates where skulls belonging to people from another time greet her. It's as if she's entered another world. Who were they when they lived? Sometimes the bones seem to be breathing. The fine hairs on her arms stick up as electricity courses up her spine. She marvels at this life force that grips her after all these years.

She passes through a second wooden gate and looks toward the kitchen door of the house.

CHAPTER 2: *Fee Fi, Fo, Fum*

*E*lena arriving, rubs a hand over her cheek, feeling more at ease in the middle room between Baba's kitchen and Dedushka Victor's workbench, where a world of birch and cedar mixes with borscht and cabbage to make a masala. But most prevalent is the smoky scent of legs of lamb and pork hanging from the ceiling and the fresh smell of the haystacks Baba keeps for her animals: three guinea pigs, some chickens, a pig, and the mean goat Koza, who's tied up in the long, narrow backyard amongst the hanging vines. Except for the guineas, who are Baba's mascots, the animals live outside—the chickens in a coop, Koza on a long leash, and Piglet, the pig, who sleeps on a dog bed in a small house.

Elena fears Dedushka Victor—or De-doo, as she refers to him affectionately—will kill Piglet one day for a special feast. She used to love and pet all these animals, but now she knows they will become food, hung out to dry like the ones hanging from the inside beams of the cabin, so she's tried to put some distance between herself and them—all except for Piglet. She has asked De-doo on several occasions to spare the pig, whom she loves as a pet and walks every day in mid-morning up Taraval on a leash.

From the middle room Elena jiggles the squeaky doorknob into Baba's kitchen but before she can open it, she hears Baba Vera dart to the door, calling, "Fee, fi, fo, fum!"

Baba still plays this game, even though it's no longer a surprise. It's as if she role-plays the big bad witch of the fairy tale to test Elena—or she's just a madwoman, which Elena increasingly suspects is the case.

"*Who is there?*" Baba opens the door wearing her red apron and brown garden boots and ushers Elena into the warm kitchen of the log-framed hut. The black iron stove is burning with red embers and a pot of soup, top boiling. Tall beef ribs stick out of the pot and salute Elena. She doesn't know where to look. The place is a mess.

This *fee, fi, fo, fum* has long been Baba's way of greeting her. It's like her signature handshake. Maybe it's her way of keeping Elena on her toes, but it doesn't scare her anymore. After years of the same greeting, she's grown used to it. Baba always knows when she's arrived. She runs around the hay on her broom, making dust, spinning the straw into a whirlpool, then orders, "Sweep it up, dearie, and do it cheery. Ha! Ha!"

Before Elena takes off her cape, she asks, "Baba, please, can you tell me about the woman visiting Father Al this morning?"

Baba squeals, swirling once again in the whirlpool of dust she's created, and the sound makes Elena jump. It reminds her of the high-pitched voice she heard this morning behind the door in Father Al's chapel. She's not surprised that Baba knows. She imagines Baba has a crystal ball and that she must know about the taxi driver too.

Baba is still spinning around. The commotion sends a small mouse out from the hay.

"Baba, tell me please about the woman," Elena asks again, but Baba just looks away, her lips twisting like a sideways S shape, and smacks her lips.

"And the man in the taxi outside Our Lady this morning?"

"He'll be back in good time, you'll see," Baba says, "and he'll take that foul woman with him."

Elena feels worried for Father Al but realizes no further information will be forthcoming from Baba on this topic, so she turns away and walks back into the middle room between De-doo's studio and the kitchen to hang her cape and take an apron. In this middle room, empty of the farm feeling, she feels steady. Meanwhile, she hears Baba gabbing away in some confusing, seemingly nonsense syllables—a gibberish Elena doesn't understand.

When she switches back to English, she yells, "You can twirl that small mouse by its tail, give him a ride, make him dizzy, put him in a tailspin, and fling him away!"

Elena wonders what the hell she's talking about. Is Baba asking her to catch the mouse with her bare hands? Or is she referring to the woman in the church, or the man in his cab? She doesn't ask; she just sets about sweeping the kitchen floor, piling up the hay, and focusing on the frame of the cabin, with its wooden logs and seamless joints—not a nail to be seen. Her concentration on the cabin structure gives order to her mind. Obviously, she can't expect Baba to make any sense.

Elena wishes De-doo were here today to help clarify for her. He translates Baba's words and helps her to make sense of things. He even teases Baba when she says weird stuff, making Elena feel understood. He's like the seamless joints in the cabin.

One day De-doo told Elena about their home. "It just passed down and down as needed, and then down to us." Another time he said it was a model of the oldest Russian house built in 1836 in Fort Ross, California. Elena knew her dedushka Victor wasn't that old—but then he, like Baba, didn't seem to have any particular age.

Another time he said he wanted to create a cabin similar to the one he lived in as a child in Russia. He couldn't remember the name of the town where he'd been born, but he knew how to work with his hands to build furniture. Elena likes to think De-doo built this cabin after the one he lived in in Russia. She can't help thinking it's just like the one in the fairy tale Vasilisa visited to get the fire.

Baba perches on the table in the kitchen, her skinny legs dangling, her striped socks rolled down and showing her knees, which are padded with the cups she uses for gardening. As Elena comes nearer, she jumps down in front of her, lands on all fours, and starts crawling around on her hands and knees. Elena knows she's looking for her guinea pigs—especially the white one, which she likes to have around during the daylight hours. Baba associates her white guinea with daylight, like in the fairy tale where a white horse and rider bring up the day.

Baba stops at the sliding ladder. She agilely maneuvers her tiny, bony frame up the rungs, hoisting herself up to a large cold storage unit. When she's level with it, she opens the door and grabs at a beef shoulder clod on the top shelf. The moist hunk of fresh meat slides out easily into her arms.

"Get to it, Girl. I'm famished. You need to slice that meat and fry it." She wobbles on the moveable ladder. "Hand me those shears." On the wall is a humongous pair of shears, stainless steel, reflecting the light. Elena frees the heavy tool from its hook, no longer surprised by its weight after having done this repeatedly. But these shears seem wrong for this job; they look more like something you'd use to cut large branches, not to snip meat.

"Here, Baba." She holds out the unyielding shears. "But tell me, how will you cut through that shoulder with these?" she says, thinking a meat knife and then a grinder would be better.

"Ahh! You are too smart; you've already learned which tools are right. But give it here." Baba takes the shears out of her hand and twirls them in the air like a baton while all the time hugging the beef clod and standing precariously on her ladder. Then she jumps down and hands the shears back to Elena, who returns them to their hook, wondering if what's just transpired is another ritual game, or another test.

Shoving her face close to Elena's, Baba says, "Now you take the shoulder and cut it, so we can fry it as flank steaks." When Elena doesn't react right away, Baba screams, "Go to it, girl—I'm hungry!"

But it seems she can't wait for the shoulder to be properly butchered and fried; Baba goes to the stove where long rib bones are boiling in the broth she makes for bone soup and stews, grabs one rib for each of her scrawny hands, and chews the bones clean. When she's done, she drops them back into the pot of water on the iron stove.

"Now get to work," Baba says. "Quit that stalling and do your work the way I showed you! I want the petite tender cut off of the top blade for my hors d'oeuvre." Baba wipes her mouth on her sleeve and rubs on past Elena on her way out to the garden.

Elena thinks of her like a feral animal—unpredictable, wild, always hungry.

Elena sighs once Baba's outside. She knows she can cut the tiny tender from the shoulder blade the way Baba showed her how to do it, but she's afraid to mess it up. She whispers a little prayer to her doll: "Kukla, please help me know which tools to use, to stay steady, and to follow the steps I've learned to remove the bone connective tissue and cut deep into the meat."

Focus and we will get this done, Elena says to herself. She takes a deep breath and exhales slowly, trying to tame her shaking. She sits at the table and rests her head on the cold slab of meat, which still smells fresh and clean. For that she is grateful.

She looks at the shears she returned to the wall, huge for her small hands and definitely the wrong tool. Baba tried to trick her again.

Elena looks to the cupboard, full of fine knives, and finds the appropriate tool. The sharp, curved knife seems to slide into the chuck primal, and soon even the petite tender is freed from the shoulder clod. After placing it on a special Baba plate, the one with the rooster handle, she cuts the orange connective tissue away and then removes an inch of fat. The knife slides along the connective tissue and frees up two tender pieces of beef. She smiles, feeling competent.

She moves deftly and silently through the room, gathering up her tools, stacking the various cuts of meat in preparation for cooking. From the open doorway, Baba yells, "I see you've removed the petite tender."

Elena's gaze swivels to her.

Baba's eyes wind around her rotating head in excitement. "And gotten down to the grandma skin." She waves her arms in the air and jumps up and down, and suddenly she is standing next to Elena, her eyes sparkling with pleasure, a smile rising on her wrinkled apple face as she sees the small steak tender separated from the shoulder blade and the skirt steak perfectly trimmed and tied in a steady shape, ready for braising.

Elena knows she's made her happy, though Baba will never praise her.

Baba takes the meat in her hands and places it near the oven, then gathers a stack of laundry piled a meter high. Like lightning, her voice changes from excitement to a thunderous roar. "Wash them and hang them out on the line behind the house," she hisses.

Handwashing De-doo's stained work clothes and heavy gardening outfits are Elena's least favorite task. Thankfully, they no longer use lye.

The sunlight on walls of the back room play dark and warm with the birchwood paneling, making it look like birch trees in a forest home. Large pots and pans hang beside the skulls of her ancestors. When Elena was young, she used to touch the bones and feel the shapes inside and out. Inside the skull was the scariest, especially around the jaw and eye sockets. What if the jaw closed on her hand or a tongue was still there? Baba didn't seem to mind her handling them; in fact, she seemed to invite her to know them. Elena imagined the bones liked her handling them—that if they could talk they might even have cooed, the way Baba hummed when she made Elena massage her tired feet, as she caressed them. Perhaps this playing with bones was a prep for butchering meat. Or maybe Baba wanted Elena to know about death.

Playing with the skulls was a way to get rid of her fear of them. She'd sit on the braided red and green rug, talking, and eventually asking, silently, who they once were. *Were you a czar? A princess? A Baba Yaga? A horseman? A stepsister?* She cycled through all the characters in her Russian fairy tales. Then, carefully, she would wrap the skulls in her woolen cape—warmed by the black iron stove, which cast a glow of embers all day—and rock the bones in her arms, imagining they were sisters and brothers.

"Hang those clothes in the sun before it sets!" Baba screeches, arousing her from her memories. "Be sure to wring Dedushka Victor's work pants tightly—and when you're done, sweep the floor. Then hang the small carpets far away from the clean laundry and beat them to death."

Elena goes out through the kitchen door and selects a short wooden paddle to beat out the dust from the rugs, knowing Baba is watching her.

"Harder, harder!" Baba yells. "Make those dust bugs fly out." She rushes on her broomstick through the door to the clotheslines with her mouth open wide to catch the chiggers. The lowering sun reflects on the critters, which seem to spill into her mouth.

Before Elena leaves this afternoon, she feels the impulse to ask once again about the man outside Our Lady, about the woman screaming at the top of her lungs, but she stops herself. Baba is looking in her eyes as a genie who could grant her wishes.

She has that special way of knowing when Elena wants to ask something, and she goads her. "Why don't you ask more questions?" the old woman demands.

"Let that be all," Elena replies. "You said yourself that those who know too much grow old too soon, Baba."

CHAPTER 3: *The Cab Driver*

Frank loved his first fare of the day, a regular called Henry O who lived in Pacific Heights. Every weekday morning, Frank looked forward to picking up Henry. The routine went like this: show up at seven fifty in front of his home and deliver him safely by eight to the financial district. Henry O thought Frank was a magician who could drive his cab over the cars, miraculously getting him to work in as little time as possible. Frank got a kick out of this. He privately thought that Henry O didn't manage his time well, but he liked the challenge—and if anyone could pull off the stunt to save the day, it was him and his little yellow cab.

Frank liked to save the day. He must have learned this from his brother, Fred, who'd saved him after their parents died.

Though Frank was only twenty-five, he'd decided to hunker down with the traditional taxi system in San Francisco and get his medallion when he started driving; he despised Uber's unprecedented numbers of drivers, and the increased traffic Uber and Lyft brought to San Francisco.

He strove to have a relationship with his clients. If this was old-fashioned, he didn't care. He gave his clients a safe place to talk if they wanted—like that strange woman with the Russian accent who he'd picked up yesterday. He'd taken her from the airport to the King George, an old San Francisco hotel known for its faded elegance—a fitting place for this strange woman, who mumbled to herself, pointed out cars zooming by like a child might, and wore an odd pink coat. She'd intrigued him with her wild, otherworldly clothes and colorful plastic bags.

When Frank pulled up to Green Street, Henry O waved from the window then dashed outside. Frank didn't know his last name. Henry O was like his daily bread. He looked forward to driving him to work and then picking him up again at five. It was always the same routine, Monday through Friday.

This morning, as was usually the case, Henry O got in and immediately began a one-sided conversation with Frank. "In ten minutes, Frank, my boss will be knocking on my door. 'You got the papers on the M case?' he'll ask. 'Hello . . . Where are you?' he'll ask me, as if I was some Martian. Then minutes later he'll go to the coffee room, certain I'm there eating breakfast on the job, ready to nail me. But really what I want to do instead of getting drilled is to stand at the Peet's cart near the museum on Third Street and watch all the pretty women order their cappuccinos, wet."

Henry O met Frank's eyes in the rearview mirror. Frank didn't mean to flash a face of disapproval, but he couldn't help himself. Henry O could be so crude.

"That's what they call the ones with lots of milk," Henry said. Frank only nodded.

"Why don't you leave your house at seven thirty instead of seven fifty?" Frank asked, but Henry O ignored the question. Frank knew he was paid to get him to work safely and quickly, not to change his behavior. And besides, when he got him to his office a minute before eight, Henry O always handed him twenty bucks.

On Van Ness, Frank saw his opportunity to push the pedal, speeding up in the left lane. If he took Bush, a one-way street that headed downtown and then onto the Bay Bridge, he might make it. Pressing the metal, he watched for cops in the rearview mirror, feeling alert and awake from the adrenaline rush he got driving for Henry O.

Henry O tapped Frank's shoulder. "We've got three minutes; hurry up!"

Frank met the challenge, reaching Market from Bush and making a right on Montgomery, ultimately putting Henry O in front of his building squarely at eight. Today, the flow of traffic had cooperated with him.

"Take this, buddy, you deserve it," Henry O said, handing him the twenty as he reached for the door to get out.

"Thank you."

"Tomorrow, then—seven fifty, and not a minute sooner," Henry O said, chuckling, before closing the door behind him.

His task successfully accomplished, Frank sighed, grateful for the smooth flow from morning drivers and the synchronized lights. He breathed deeply and let out a loud *ohm*. The fare, with its twenty-dollar tip, added to his elation.

Geary Boulevard took him on past the theaters and hotels where he sometimes picked up a random passenger. In front of the St. George Hotel stood a waving woman. He felt a pang of hunger, as he hadn't eaten any breakfast, but he pulled to a stop in front of the hotel. It was the Russian woman from yesterday, the one he'd picked up at SFO. *I'd recognize her anywhere.*

She was standing in the same place he'd let her off yesterday wearing more or less the same outfit, including the babushka thing on her head. She opened the door and got in, saying, "Thirty-six and Geary."

Frank headed west on Geary toward the Avenues, remembering his hunger, thinking he'd catch a breakfast at Louis' at the ocean after he dropped her off. His plans rambled on in his head until he heard her ask, "Do you know where the Russian church is?" She clearly didn't remember who he was, or that he'd taken her to the George the previous day.

Just as well. The woman had a clownish, mask-like face with zigzag eyebrows penciled across a rippled forehead. Her nose slanted in a steep slope with a ski mogul in the middle. It scared him a little. Her mouth was smeared with magenta lipstick; there was a wart on her neck and there were hairs on her chin. How had he not noticed her bizarre face yesterday? A green kerchief sat, lopsided, on her neck. Now he saw hair dyed jet black.

She stared at him. "The Russian church," she repeated.

He stammered, "Yes—the one on Geary, not at 36th?"

She held his eyes. "No! I want to go to the smaller Russian church, the one with the blue onion dome. I'm meeting someone there. Do you know that one?"

He nodded. "Still three more miles."

She was in a hurry; he could feel her vibrations coming from behind him. He imagined her shaking her foot on the back floor. He crossed Stanyan and continued west, passing restaurants and small businesses.

Finally, the woman smiled. Seeming assured, she turned her face from him, showing him her profile. Watching in the rearview mirror, he examined her nose more critically, thinking it looked more like a boxer's beaten schnozzle than a ski slope. He kept sneaking glances at her green and pink check scarf, tied in a clumsy knot at her neck, and wondering where in hell she came from, as he drove.

"There it is, there it is!" she shouted, pointing to the large church on Geary—the Holy Virgin Cathedral, not the one with the blue dome. It had a golden dome.

"You wanted the one with the blue dome, didn't you?" He looked in the rearview mirror and saw her nod. "Wait up," he said.

"Yes," she said, simmering down. He drove a few blocks more before pulling up to the curb in a quieter neighborhood in front of the blue-domed building, which looked more like a house than a church. She opened the door and nearly flew out before he'd even asked for the fare.

"Eighteen dollars," he yelled after her, but she was already rushing to the door of the church.

She stopped in her tracks, then backtracked and handed him fifty bucks, looking flustered. "Wait for me," she said.

Frank examined the fifty-dollar bill. "How long will you be?"

"If I'm more than a half hour, come in and get me," she said. "And can you be on the clock for me today? I have some important stops to make after this one." She was heading for the door.

"Look—" But before he could finish, she was safely inside the Byzantine building and the door had closed behind her. When he looked back at the passenger seat, he saw an oilcloth bag decorated with purple flowers on the seat, the triangular head scarf sticking out. She intended to keep him waiting for her.

He moved restlessly in his seat, reclining the back so he could relax. Then he turned off the meter, turned on the country western station, and zoned out, staring at his cell, only noticing his surroundings outside the cab when a white cape caught his attention.

The person wearing it was a young girl with a red sack slung over her shoulder. The modestly funny outfit made him think he was dreaming, and his eyelids drooped. Then he remembered the woman in the church and looked at his watch. It was nine thirty; a half-hour had passed since she'd entered the church.

He switched off the radio and got out, looking around. The street was unusually quiet. The girl was gone.

In the vestibule, he knocked on the door. He waited, and then he knocked again. A thin man in a black cassock with long graying hair opened the door, invited him inside, and motioned him to sit in the rear of the chapel. While the priest headed toward the altar in the front of the church, Frank examined the relics and icons of an orthodox religion, virgins and babies squeezed together like a Klimt painting. He half expected to see the odd woman squeezing herself into one of the paintings, but she was nowhere to be seen. The church was empty of parishioners and pretty empty in general, except for the fragrance of incense. Unlike other churches he'd visited, there were no benches set up with kneeling rests, only a few seats scattered about.

The robed man with the long hair disappeared behind the altar. Frank heard another door close. Amidst the religious icons and the incense, he heard two voices speaking in heated conversation. He moved closer to the altar to hear. It seemed the priest was talking to the woman.

"I don't buy it, Anya."

"I'll say it again since you don't seem to hear me," she said. "Fifteen years ago. "

"I'm not so sure of that."

"Of course it was me."

"In all this time you've been standing here, you've given me no proof."

"She's mine."

"Not a stitch of proof!" the priest repeated.

"I want her back now!" Frank heard some thuds, like maybe she was stamping her feet. "It's my right." Her voice raised a notch. "She's my daughter."

"Not so sure," the man said again.

"It was for her own good that I left her here with you."

"And it's for her own good that I continue to parent her," the man said loudly.

Frank heard a louder thunk and imagined the woman kicking something.

"Furthermore, it's for her own good now that you not see her," the priest said. "She's squared away and will not benefit from your interference. She's a special child and has her own life. I will not let you interfere. Now get out, and don't come back."

"I just want her to know that I'm back. I want to meet her. I'm her mother, for God's sake."

"*I* am her parent," he said, more forcefully. "Now please leave. I can't help you."

There was a long silence. Frank moved onto the altar, straining to hear the woman's response, careful not to hit these religious icons that seemed to be witnessing the conversation with him.

"Then . . ."

But Frank couldn't hear the rest. He imagined her twisted face with the zigzagging eyebrows across a furrowed brow. His curiosity piqued, he wondered where she'd been for all these years—and why come back for your child after fifteen years? Or was she lying about the whole thing, as the priest was clearly implying?

"I beg of you to ask her if she wants to see her mother," the woman persisted.

"You don't understand. The girl believes she doesn't have parents." Then he repeated himself, showing the patience and restraint of a priestly man, as was his station: "I am her parent and have been caring for her for fifteen years."

"What is her name?"

"I'm sorry, I cannot help you. Please leave."

Shrieks, sounding like wild whooping coyotes, filled the incense-filled church. Then Frank heard footsteps. The priest was ushering her out of his chamber behind the altar.

Frank hurried toward the back of the church, then turned to watch the scene unfold.

The priest was escorting her toward the door. Her face was smeared with black mascara and magenta lipstick. She looked ghoulish. The priest looked into Frank's face as they passed him. It seemed to him the man was silently asking him to take her off the premises. He tapped Frank's shoulder gently and with his eyes seemed to confirm she was a madwoman, but all he said was, "Good luck. Be careful."

Frank walked out to his cab with the woman and opened the door for her as she yelled at the priest, "I'll be back! Don't you think you can get rid of me!"—then spat in the direction of the church.

Frank didn't like that at all and considered what he'd gotten himself into by agreeing to drive the woman for the day. It wasn't too late to say no, though, was it? He looked toward the priest in apology but the man had already disappeared into his church.

The woman got into the back seat. Her body moved disjointedly, as if her arms and legs were doing the mash; it reminded Frank of a dance he'd seen characters on *The Simpsons* do when he was a kid. She started blabbering in her mother tongue—harsh, chirping tones he didn't understand and then low tones like a monster, all of which culminated in a howl.

That, he understood.

When she began to settle he heard her sobbing and handed her a box of tissue from the front seat. Then he waited, watching the closed door to the church, half-hoping the priest would come out and redo the ending. Frank didn't like what had just transpired, regardless of who had the moral authority.

Then he felt a sharp finger poking the back of his neck.

He turned, met her eyes, and saw a softer face. Some of the tension must have been dispelled with the cry. Or she was one of those people who had multiple personalities, changing their behavior on a dime. That thought unnerved him, but he felt sorry for her too. It was clear she'd lost her child. The priest had acknowledged as much. The girl indeed existed—he'd seen her—and the priest had parented her all these years.

He decided he could sacrifice his late breakfast at Louis' to take this woman to her next destination. For some reason, he felt protective toward the girl. Maybe because the woman was so strange. Maybe because the girl had been saved by the priest. Maybe because he himself had lost his own parents and been saved in a similar way by his older brother. He thought he might get more information, and maybe he'd even report back to the priest what he discovered.

"Where to?"

She bit her lip. "Just drive, please." She thrust a handful of bills at him.

Frank took them—more fifties—nodded, turned on the meter, and left the Russian church, thinking to return her to the King George via Golden Gate Park. She didn't say anything.

As he drove, he watched her in the rearview mirror. Her eyes were lowered; her breathing had come to rest. He drove past the uphill parking lot toward the restaurant on the cliff, staring out at the waves crashing over Seal Rock and listening to the barking sea lions, thinking again about the bacon and eggs he wouldn't have.

"I used to come here," the woman said in her thick accent, breaking the silence. She was looking out the front window with her crooked smile at the lacy shoreline. "My uncle used to love to bring me here to hear the sea lions and watch the waves."

Frank listened to her rolled r's and mixed v's and w's while looking at the crashing waves ahead on Ocean Beach, an uneasy feeling in his gut. He knew she was off. In fact, she went on and on about being from this neighborhood, saying, "*Tzis vere* I grew up," though it was clear that she was from Russia. She told him she went to public school on 38th and Balboa and then to the middle school on Anza. Then she stopped as if to recall something from long ago, and he heard her ruffling pages as if she were checking something.

He knew everything about this neighborhood because he'd actually grown up here, graduated from high school less than ten years ago. The middle school wasn't on Anza; the high school wasn't on 38th, either. This was his hood. Either she'd forgotten or was lying. He looked in the back seat again and saw she was on the phone, talking to someone in Russian.

She looked up at him and asked if he could find a restroom. He turned left across the Great Highway, entered Golden Gate Park, and pulled up to a public restroom.

When the woman got out of the cab, a San Francisco guidebook fell from her coat pocket. She picked it up quickly and left for the restroom. What an enigma she was.

When she returned from the bathroom, she looked refreshed; she'd washed the mascara off her face and reapplied magenta lipstick. Now she didn't have that pasted look of a woman hiding behind a mask. She asked him if he could take her around to a few places. She wanted to see the bison and the Japanese Tea Garden, and then, before returning to the George, she wanted to make one last stop on Taraval Street to visit her sister.

When he agreed to her requests, she looked him squarely in the eyes and said, "You must wonder about me?"

"I'm curious, yes." He thought about the confusion between her story and the priest's and how she really didn't know the neighborhood as she claimed. His own brain was wandering a crooked line and he wanted to get it straight. And did she really have a sister in San Francisco or was that a universal sister, as in "the sisterhood"?

"Then you have family here?" he inquired, now curious about a possible sister.

"A fraternal twin." She wrinkled her nose and stuck out her tongue. "I just returned to the Bay Area after some time away. I came to reclaim Vasilisa." Her eyes grew bigger in their sockets. "You heard my conversation with the priest, yes?"

"Some of it, yes."

"What did you hear?" she asked.

"Not much," Frank lied.

"I saw you as we were leaving the sanctuary. You were listening. Tell me."

"I heard you asking for your daughter."

Again she started talking in Russian, as if she were talking to the gods. He didn't understand, and he didn't like the way she kept flipping back and forth between languages when he clearly couldn't understand what she was saying.

Finally, she quieted, and then said, "Yes, I came back to San Francisco to find my daughter." She looked to him as if studying him, trying to read him. "I had to get out of town. Someone was threatening me and my baby. To protect her, I had to leave her. The only safe place I knew was the church. Now I want her back."

"Look, I'm sorry for your loss," he said, but he still wasn't sure he believed her. She certainly wasn't trustworthy. She wasn't just odd, she was a wacko. Instead his allegiance fell to the girl in the white cape, whom he'd determined to be the daughter in question. He would need to find out more.

"Anya, my name is Anya Prokioff," she said.

"Frank Hudson," he replied.

She told him a long story about how she had immigrated to the US from Russia as a child in 1965, going on and on in a mechanical way that made it hard to listen. She looked older than her stated age, Frank thought, and she wouldn't have that thick accent if she'd lived here as a child. He figured she must be at least sixty-five now, which made it unlikely that the girl was hers. Had she really had a baby at fifty and left her behind in the church fifteen years ago?

"Why did you leave your baby?" he asked.

She didn't answer, just looked out the window at the tall trees lining the street and asked him to take her to the bison as if the answer would be there in the dung.

He pulled onto JFK, heading east toward the field.

"Look," he said, "I don't mean to pry. I'm sorry." He thought of his own mother, and of his father. Fred had protected him so lovingly after their deaths. Frank had been just eight years old at the time.

Frank sat quietly, thinking about his own life, and then wondering if the girl was really Anya's daughter. He wanted to hear her story. But he'd have to be cool and not get in her face.

As they neared the bison paddock, he remembered how as a boy he'd stare for hours at the fenced acreage, marveling at the animals, tracing their compact shapes in his mind, running his eyes over their mysterious humps, imagining they were filled with water. He contemplated the stories he studied in fourth grade geography of buffalo sacrifices. The stories always included some princess. He used to watch eagerly for a sight of the princess and he guessed he was doing that now, but the only fairy tale figure he saw in the mirror was the ugly stepmother, sitting in the back seat of his car. He shivered and rolled up the window against the creeping fog, fearing for the princess she claimed was her daughter.

"Stop here," Anya said.

Frank pulled over and she got out, crossed JFK, and stood by the twelve-foot fence, leaving him to contemplate further. Why had he agreed to drive this woman? Now he was mixed up in a different fairy tale, imagining her as a witch, reciting, *Mirror, mirror on the wall, who's the fairest of them all?* into his rearview mirror. How had he actually decided to drive a cab at all? Hadn't he always wanted to be an archaeologist, traveling to far-off lands to solve mysteries? Or an artist, drawing the shapes of things?

He watched Anya across Kennedy Drive, staring at the bison through the fence. It was as if she were trying to communicate with them. One of the smaller ones walked toward her until a mother buffalo nudged him off the fence and they both ran away. What in hell was she doing?

When she got back in, she sat in the passenger seat beside him. Her thinning, wind-blown hair tossed across her face, she sat silently as he accelerated toward the Japanese Tea Garden.

When he pulled up to the garden, she didn't get out; instead, she directed him to continue on to Taraval Street. He drove down Tea Garden Lane, away from the de Young Museum and toward the Avenues on the Sunset side of the park.

Does she really have a sister on Taraval? he wondered.

"I want to go via the scenic route," she said as he turned onto 19th.

"No, we're almost there now," he said, and continued south. He tried to draw more information out of her. "Your daughter's name is Vasilisa?"

"What I want to do is figure out how I can find her." There was a bite to her answer.

"Is that why you're going to Taraval?"

She didn't answer.

The more Frank thought about the girl he'd seen that morning, the more he wanted to find her and talk to her. But it wasn't his place. What would he say—*I think I might have been driving your mother all around the city today? Did you know you were adopted?* He could ruin the girl's life.

"I want to see the gorillas, go on," Anya shouted as they neared Taraval.

"No zoo today," Frank said. "Have you seen a lawyer?" he asked, changing the subject toward what he wanted to talk about.

She looked toward him, her eyebrows raised in question. "A lawyer!" She laughed hysterically.

"Yeah, a lawyer and not a mountain gorilla, for God's sake." *Shit!*

She looked like she'd just dropped in from some other planet, maybe Mars. Maybe Martians wore green kerchiefs and flowered oilcloth bags and had smeared lips, jagged brows, and sloped noses. The way she'd howled at the priest in the little church and spat at him, the way she'd thrown all those fifties at Frank—all of it seemed now like poop, poop, poop to him. She was pooping, leaving her shit all over the place, and now she was laughing like a fucking crazy woman.

And what did he know about this woman who said she'd given up her child fifteen years ago and now wanted her back? And why did he care? And why the hell was he feeling so judgmental?

Shit happens. That he knew. Fred had raised him, become both his mother and father, after their parents died. Much older than his younger brother, circumstances had forced a youth to raise a kid who was always crying for his mom, always asking, "Why'd she leave me?" Fred had been tough, but fair. He'd kept them in the same house with the same routine, up and out of the house at 8:00 a.m., downhill to the elementary school on Anza with a lunchbox in hand.

Frank considered the priest—how he'd raised this child, this girl, also by circumstance, and was now protecting her from a madwoman. For Frank, the man in the cassock was his brother, and he was the little girl.

He now felt sure: He had to protect her from this lunatic.

CHAPTER 4: Dusk

*E*lena grabs her white cape and kisses Baba goodbye on her hairy chin. She feels pride at having met the tasks Baba set out—tasks that seemed impossible at first but were doable with the help of her doll. She loves this part of the day, when she walks from the hideaway on Taraval Street and eventually crosses into Golden Gate Park, letting the woods of pine and oak seep into her.

At dusk, when everything softens and the great shadows of the big trees seem to support her, she enters a vast darkness. Yet the woods shimmer with the bright light of the moon or the orange-red sunset sky that shines through the trees and reflects off the ponds—all silvery and pink faintly glimmering through the tremulous, watery fields. She's at home with the sun setting over her left shoulder; the deepening grey-blue sky, the prelude to the night, suits her. She listens to the quietest part of the day before it turns to sleep.

Her white cape alerts occasional cars to her presence like a safety vest. She moves into the park with stealth, grateful for all the animal games she's learned from Baba and the ways of observation Father Al taught her as a child when they walked hand-in-hand across the park.

In addition to her cape, her doll, tucked in her pocket, protects her from danger. She squeezes her. *All is well*, she tells herself. She walks on quietly and at peace, alert to the energy, the great web of roots, rising from the ground through her feet and expanding through her body.

With nightfall, her vision adjusts to the dark and her hearing and sense of smell seem more acute. The eucalyptus with their peeling bark add streaks of white to the forest mix, nourishing her with their fragrance. The oaks, her favorite, provide a thick carpet of moist mulch to cushion each step.

Sometimes even the smell of a dead animal picks her up, for it, too, offers a reminder of life. Life touches her everywhere as she walks through the mulch. Rats and mice run over and under the soft mulch carpet, and the adorable mole looks so much like a seal with its velvety coat. She tastes the earthy essence of the forest in this urban park that stretches for miles across to the Pacific Ocean. She imagines that this used to be sand dunes and she's walking in a converted seabed, which thrills her.

She stops at the pond on Middle Drive, as is her custom, and sits on its edge to feed a flock of ducks with the dried bread she carries in her red shoulder bag. The littlest duck always lags behind. Elena worries about her, fearing she will be lost from her family or be eaten. *Be careful, won't you?* she entreats the duck silently. Her body shakes in some mysterious premonition as she envisions the death of the fledgling.

The little duck swims toward her outstretched hand and pecks at the crumbs. Elena listens to the lapping of the water, meeting the edge of the pond, and as she does she hears a soft whisper which she knows to be a human sound—a slight *shh*, a sweet whistling sound. Was this meant to alert her?

Suddenly she realizes she's not alone. Someone stands quietly at a distance, watching her—a small, thin man. He's close enough that she can hear him, but his relaxed demeanor tells her he means no harm. With the reflection of the setting sun shining on his long hair, he seems as natural as the dusk.

She knows right away that it's the taxi driver. Why has he shown up here? Before she can make sense of anything, he's gone. She's surprised to have seen him again and she wonders at this coincidence.

Still wondering, she continues home. Upon arriving at the church, Elena quietly opens the door and walks into the small foyer. The shadows of the holy icons flicker in the candlelight, following her to the kitchen.

She finds Father Al sitting at the table, guarding a clay dish holding two golden piroshki, meat-filled turnovers, and a bowl of purple soup covered in saran wrap. After placing them in the oven, he looks toward her. His eyes rest on her face, his lips turned upward, showing his natural kindness.

"Hello, Father Al," she says, placing her cape on a hanger.

"Sit down, you must be hungry."

She sits and they wait ten minutes for the timer to beep on the oven. She enjoys this natural time of silence with Father Al.

Once the food is ready, he bows his head and prays, "Thank You, Dear Lord, for the food we are about to receive. And, Dear Father, for this daughter you loaned me. Amen."

"Thank you, Father Al," she says. She raises a spoonful of purple soup to her lips. "This is delicious," she says, thinking how grateful she is for this father who cares for her, who has instilled in her a sense of ease. She loves how he waits for her return to eat dinner, how readily he accepts her and listens to her. She trusts him.

They sit in silence and eat until she says, "Father, will you tell me about the woman who visited this morning? I heard her."

He grimaces slightly. "Yes, she was loud, wasn't she?"

"Why did she come here?"

"She needs help," he says. "She's misdirected in her ways." He takes a forkful of piroshki into his mouth.

Elena senses he's holding back something—but maybe it's a priest thing not to divulge the sins of others. It seemed that the woman was demanding something. Or was she simply confessing her sins in a blaming way?

He chews slowly. She takes a spoonful of soup.

"Has she come to you for help?"

"Yes, that is it."

"And the man waiting for her?"

"A public cabbie is all. Poor man! We spoke briefly in passing this morning. She has hired him to take her around."

"Oh!"

"He's innocent of her antics." He laughs. "I'm not sure who is taking whom for a ride, though." The conversation lightens up and Elena feels better.

"I saw him twice today," she explains. "Once in the morning and then again in the park this evening. It surprised me to see him there at the duck pond."

"Yes, child, that is strange." Father Al looks down at his soup.

"I wonder if it's just a coincidence or . . . something to do with that woman."

Elena wants an answer but when none is forthcoming, she puts this mystery into the "not knowing" category, the same place as the many other mysteries she accepts.

"There is one more thing, Father. Did you tell Baba about the woman?"

"Baba knows of her," is all he says.

They finish their meal in silence. Once again Elena is aware of Baba's keen ability to know things. It's not that she can really fly on her broom or be in two places at once, but she does have an inexplicable awareness of everything that occurs in Elena's life.

Elena wonders once again if she has a crystal ball, or just more generally the ability to foresee.

When Father Al leaves for the chapel for his evening prayers, Elena runs her fingers across her little doll—just three inches tall—touching the tiny silken crown of her head, her silk shoes, and the lacy apron wrapped around her waist. She pats her left hand, dips a little finger into a cup of water, and brings it to the doll's tiny mouth.

Oh, Kukla, he really didn't tell me if he told Baba about the woman's visit, did he? Because if he'd said he'd told her, like on the phone, then I would know Baba doesn't have a crystal ball or something like ESP.

After washing and drying the plates and silverware, she puts them in the cabinet and listens to Father Al chanting *Kyrie Eleison*, over and over, attending to the rising and the falling of the notes as if they are gentle raindrops.

Her eyelids become heavy. Sleepily, she walks the narrow stairwell to her attic room and climbs into bed, where she falls fast asleep.

The next morning she wakes to the dawn of a new day, relaxed and joyful as the dream escapes into the dust mites, leaving only a gentle breeze as it passes.

Father Al's waiting for her at the door with a plate of biscuits and tea when she comes downstairs. His eyes search her face with his intelligent and priestly look. He's wearing his long black cassock and hat; he's about to give weekday mass for his few parishioners.

"Thank you, Father," she says, taking the tea and biscuits. "It's a beautiful day, isn't it?"

"Yes, Elena. You look rested this morning after your long day yesterday."

"That woman is not here," she says. "I'm relieved."

"I am too, child." He exits the kitchen, leaving her alone.

She sits in the kitchen to drink her tea and eat her biscuits, then leaves Our Lady, ready for her weekday training sessions with Baba Vera.

There is no cab sitting out front today.

CHAPTER 5: *Anya, Is That You?*

*A*t Anya's direction, Frank pulled up to an old, dilapidated storefront that looked like it had been closed for decades. In fact, it looked dead, like nothing was happening inside.

Anya got out. "Give me thirty minutes," she said, and pushed the bell.

Moments later, a tiny old woman—or it could have been a skinny child with bony knees and striped stockings—appeared in the crack of the door. She squinted at the bright light and looked up at Anya, and her fingers crossed over her mouth, covering a gasp.

"Is that you, Anya?"

Anya stepped forward and the tiny woman directed her inside the dark storefront.

The wooden door from another era slammed shut, and soon after that Frank thought he heard his passenger wailing again, but he couldn't be sure.

After she was inside, he got out and walked toward a side passageway. It was ten forty-five. He would knock on the front door in thirty minutes, then return her to the George and be free of her by noon.

He jiggled the latch and opened the wooden side gate slowly, so as not to call attention to himself, hoping he would find a bench or chair to sit on where he could wait and munch on some trail mix he kept in his pocket.

What he saw was a long, narrow passageway about three feet wide and thirty feet long, bordered on one side by the brown shingled house and on the other by a tall wooden fence made of two-by-fours and topped with pointed spires. The zigzag pattern reminded him of Anya's eyebrows.

At the end of the passageway was a second wooden gate. Several skulls hung on the side of the fence. He shivered. *What is this place? What the hell!* When he got closer, he looked up to see more clearly. *These are real skulls! Shit!* He remembered Henry O telling him once about how certain people worshiped their ancestors; how in a remote village in Peru he'd met a family that had skulls going generations back sitting on their mantles, blessing them.

Frank shook his head. His hands felt tingly and his head woozy. He moved away from the skulls and walked toward the second gate. He jiggled the latch but the door was locked from the inside. In order to open it, he would have to scale it.

Instead, he walked close to the house and stopped between two narrow windows. Their shades were pulled, but there was a slit down the side of one. He peeked through, but it was dark inside. Flat up against the house with his back on the siding, he slid down to sit and wait, munching on some nuts while cold fog from the coast spilled over him.

His stomach growled. He hadn't eaten breakfast and now the nuts were just reminding him of how hungry he was. He pictured the woman's babushka, the pink coat, the big nose, her demands to stop the cab at the bison field, and the way the calf and its mother had bolted from her.

He heard sounds from inside the small house—plumbing or heating sounds, maybe? Scraping of tools, shuffling of feet. A pot. A hammer. What was going on?

His stomach growled again, turning into a sleek pain. Suddenly, he had to go to the bathroom—and fast. He looked at the fence again, but if he scaled it, then what? He'd only be in the backyard.

He reluctantly but hurriedly knocked on the house's front door.

Footsteps shuffled toward the door. It opened.

"Yes?" said a small, round man wearing a carpenter apron with a hammer, screwdriver, pliers, and a plane visible in its pockets. Lines swirled his face like a labyrinth, ending up circling his tiny pink mouth. Down the sides of his face lived deeper crevices.

"I'm her cab driver," Frank said. "Please, I need to use the toilet. I got to go."

The man nodded and moved aside. "Come in."

Frank entered the dark house made of logs—stuck together, it seemed, without nails—and walked toward the door on the left wall where the man gestured. He turned the knob to find a small light-filled bathroom with knotty pine two-by-fours with round circles staring at him.

He sat down and heard voices.

"Get out of here, you witch," a woman said from another room.

Frank stayed on the pot and put his ear close to the wall and listened.

"Ahh! Those old spells again, is it?" said a man's voice. Frank assumed it was the man who had let him in.

"You stay out of this, Victor, this is between me and Anya," the woman said. "Be quiet. You do not know the way."

Frank pushed his ear closer to the wall. Once he was done, he stood up and flushed the toilet slowly—cringing, since the last thing he wanted was to be heard. He put the cover down, opened the door gently, and walked into the large log room, glad to leave behind the eyes of the knotty pine, glowing like onions in the sun.

The pink coat rested on a hand-carved armchair. The babushka on the floor. Two carpenter benches lined the wall and the shelves above them held tools—hammers, grinders, circular drills, chisels, boxes of nails and screws, utility tape, and hand-saws. On the far side of the room and to his left was another door. He opened it and moved into a sparsely furnished room with birch paneling. A coat rack held a white cape and a red shoulder bag. The girl's! He felt the rush of panic. What was going on here? Had the woman known the girl was here all along?

"You killed her mother with that curse of yours!" The same woman's voice, not Anya's—lacking Anya's distinctive way of rolling her l's into each other and putting z's in where they weren't.

"You took *ze* girl. I want her." This time it was Anya, Frank could tell her voice anywhere.

Frank was confused now. So Anya had been lying. She wasn't the girl's mother. And worse—she'd killed the girl's mother? He now imagined her to be a beast, a monster, from another world. He heard scraping and grinding sounds. The door was slightly ajar. He peeked inside to a see wooden floor covered with hay. It looked to him like a field. A broom. A rake.

The other woman, who had the largest eyes he'd ever seen and wore striped knee socks and kneepads, picked up the broom, twirled it, and pushed it into Anya. Frank's eyes widened as he realized these two old women were fighting.

Anya kicked a small black dog—or was it another kind of animal?—and lunged toward the woman holding the broom, grabbing her around the waist, fighting and kicking.

"How dare you come here!" cried the woman with the broom. "Don't you know I'll guard the girl with my life? I'll kill you first."

A fog of sorts suddenly seemed to fill the room, only not the kind Frank was used to seeing in San Francisco. He didn't know whether it was Anya taking a blow with the other woman rising above her, or his own fog clouding his view.

"Calm yourselves, Vera, Anya," the man said in a steady tone.

Then the door opened fully and the man appeared beside Frank.

"Would you like a glass of water?" he asked, holding out a full cup.

"Thank you." Frank gulped the water.

The man shut the door behind him, then passed in front of Frank and moved to the middle of the room. Frank followed.

"Two cats," the man said.

"Will they be alright?" Frank asked.

"Old business. That's all."

"Should I wait for her?'

"No," the man said, ushering him outside.

Frank heard Anya squeal. He imagined her being held down by the other woman's broom. Should he leave? What with the noises, the threats and yelling, and the final image of one of them rising up like a bird or a ghost? He shook himself.

Should he call the cops?

After what Frank saw and heard, he was shaking—but more, he wondered where the girl was. Seeing her cape and bag in that house worried him. Was she inside? Had she witnessed what he had? Was she in danger?

He didn't feel comfortable getting into his car and driving away, but he wanted to scram. His hands were trembling and his knees felt like they might buckle, so he left the cab in front of the house and started walking—past the side gate, where he'd waited earlier, and toward the corner. At the corner, he stopped—and in the pause, he saw her a couple of blocks down Taraval, walking slowly in his direction with some sort of small animal, not a dog, on a leash.

He was curious and relieved when she turned a corner. He didn't want her to see him, to think that he was stalking her.

He turned back to his car and saw Anya's bag and kerchief on the backseat.

He was suddenly terrified that the girl might run into Anya. He needed to whisk that woman away from this place.

He was all about getting Anya away from the girl now. He knocked on the door. Victor opened the door again. The two men looked at each other.

"I'm here to get her out of here," Frank said, looking toward the coat rack with the cape and red sack.

The man nodded, turned, and said in a clear voice, "Your taxi's leaving, Anya."

Frank waited outside, standing by the cab.

The man emerged from the house with Anya on his arm and her coat and babushka held at his opposite side. He walked her out and into the cab and closed the door, and then he sighed.

Frank sighed too—with relief—and moved to the driver's side.

To the George, the unspoken destination.

CHAPTER 6: *Wild Duck*

his morning, Elena looks down from the dormer of the attic room at the cab driver she saw at the duck pond last evening. He seems to have business at the church again.

From above, he looks smaller than she remembers. She stares at his shiny hair, cinched in a ponytail; his nose, too prominent and large for his face, looks like an isosceles from this distance. He wears a day-old beard like he didn't have time to shave today. His black hair, pulled back tight, exposes dark brown eyes, curvy eyebrows, and a wide forehead. His jeans and plaid shirt are simple and clean. He stands by his car door waiting, holding a plastic water bottle, staring at the door of the church and seeming to contemplate whether to go in. He rubs his chin and pulls at his beard between taking sips of water, and then he turns and faces the cab as if he's remembered something.

Elena walks down from her attic room to the vestibule. Father Al must be in his chambers. In the small kitchen near his office she takes a morning bun from the counter and listens. He seems to be alone. Unlike yesterday she hears no voices. After placing the bun in her bag, she slips into her cape and leaves the vestibule.

The woman isn't here, so why is the cab driver? She understands there's some connection between the two of them, but she doesn't know what it is.

He's sitting in his cab when she walks outside. She passes in front of him, crossing to the other side of the cab, then stops. He doesn't see her, engrossed as he is with his radio receiver. She walks closer to him, on his side of the cab, and peers inside. There is a shiny floral-print bag on the seat with a green scarf sticking out of it. *Odd! The woman must be inside the church.*

She hears clacking and static sounds on the radio receiver. He seems to be waiting for the dispatcher. She listens.

He says into the receiver, "Yeah, I'm here on the Avenues . . . related to that passenger from yesterday . . . waiting. Her stuff."

"Get rid of her," comes a raspy voice. "She's the passenger from hell, Frank."

When he signs off, Elena is still standing there. She looks at him. "Frank," she repeats. The cab driver has a name now and that pleases her. "Are you waiting for someone?" she asks.

Startled at first, he can't seem to answer her.

"Excuse me. Why are you here?" she asks.

Frank looks up at her.

"Tell me, please, if you're waiting for that woman, the one who was here yesterday?"

Elena doesn't know what to make of this man. He's young, courteous enough. Concerned—perhaps holding some message deep inside him? Is he here to see her? To speak with Father Al about "the passenger from hell"? A cat's got his tongue. He's not answering her. She feels comforted that the man's boss called the woman "the passenger from hell." That fits with Father Al's assessment of her too.

"No, I'm not waiting for her. Yesterday afternoon I dropped her at her hotel; I'm done with her."

He looks deeply at Elena with warm eyes. She senses he wants to tell her something, so she waits.

"Her name is Anya," he says. "She's from Russia. She has a sister here."

Elena moves closer. She hopes he'll say more.

"She's strange and I don't trust her," he continues. "I think she's whacked out."

"Whacked out?" Elena wants to know more.

"It's her intentions," he explains.

Elena raises her eyebrows.

"She's up to no good. I just saw a wicked fight between her and her sister."

Elena shivers at the idea of another woman like her and says, "Please, tell Father Al what you know."

"She left something in my taxi." He points to the backseat.

"Oh," Elena says, as if surprised, though she's already seen the bag. It looks to her like the ones the newly arrived Russian immigrants carry to the markets on Geary Boulevard.

"Why would you bring it here to Father Al?" she asks, a bit miffed. She fears the taxi man will bring the woman back here and Father Al will have to see her again.

"The priest seems to know her," he says.

"He doesn't want her stuff," Elena tells him. "She's loud and misdirected, foul—and the passenger from hell." She shoots him a little half-smile.

"You overheard." The cab driver smiles now too. "I'm just here to leave this with Father Al. I didn't want to see her again."

"Do you know what she wants?" Elena asks.

"She's looking for her child. . . ." Frank seems to consider whether to say more. "She says she left a baby and she wants her back."

"Her child?"

"Yeah, that's what all this is about—a child she gave up fifteen years ago."

Elena feels a jolt and steadies herself, puts her hand in her pocket, knowing the woman is here for her. But who is she? Surely not her mother. It occurs to her that she might be in danger. She grips Kukla tight in her hand.

"Why were you at the duck pond last evening?"

"I often go there at dusk," he says. "I live in the neighborhood, that's all."

She looks at him. She's not afraid of him. He seems like an ally. But with nothing further to say, she turns and walks away from him.

She feels his eyes following her. She senses he's there for her, has her back regarding the misdirected woman who's looking for her. She wishes that Father Al would trust her enough to tell her what's going on. Is this how he protects her? She caresses her doll and contemplates the appearance of the cab driver, the mystery of this woman, and her effect on Father Al. She walks downhill toward the park. The onion-domed church and the man recede with each step toward her Baba Yaga.

Entering the park at 36th Avenue she saunters by the lake where seagulls and terns play. The trees stand steady and grounded; Elena feels at home here. She dallies as she crosses JFK and Middle Drive and finally finds her way onto 25th Avenue. She follows the cars south, crossing the ABC streets to Taraval.

She enters through the side passage of the Taraval house and hears Baba whirling around inside. Her arrival always excites Baba. Elena imagines her watching through a slit in the drawn shades as she passes along the side of De-doo's shop. *They're watching me now. I feel their eyes—but they are kind eyes, especially De-doo's.*

As is her custom, Baba does not let Elena spy on her. It's the other way around.

Baba's in front of her before she arrives and it's not the first time. For the millionth time, Elena suspects Baba knows things are going to happen before they happen.

"*Fee, fi, fo, fum*, I smell . . ."

But today, Baba doesn't finish; she says instead, "Today will be different! A new task for you, my dearie! Do it cheery."

Elena knows that despite her goading, Baba wants to see her succeed, and that's why she pushes her to do new and different tasks—to push her forward. She's a taskmaster and seems to have a plan for Elena.

What next? Elena thinks. *Never a dull moment here.*

"Where is Red?" Baba yells. "Are you here, Red? *Fee, fi, fo, fum!*"

A bushel of newly mown hay piled six inches high on the kitchen and family room floor makes the whole house smell like a field, and everything is in greater disarray than it was yesterday when she left with Piglet. Sweeping is one of Elena's tasks, and she wonders why Baba and De-doo have to make it so hard for her. The animals must have been fighting, spewing the hay in all directions.

Then she remembers what the cab driver said—*I just saw a wicked fight between her and her sister*—and suddenly, she knows. Anya came here yesterday and fought with Baba. The horrifying realization that Baba is the madwoman's sister alarms her enough to make her go limp. Feeling faint, she bends toward the floor and touches it. *Baba and Anya, sisters! No way!* The revelation shocks her to her core. What if Anya's claim to be her mother is true? This thought makes her buckle inside so that all seems inside-out and scattered, the way Baba takes off her clothes all inside-out and Elena has to make them right.

Anya can't be my mother, she assures herself, holding her doll. *But I must stay on my toes.*

Baba chases the three guinea pigs with a broom. The red one and the white one scurry with the energy of daylight while the black one lags behind, using his whiskers to feel where he is going as if he can't see.

"He'll wake up with the dark," Baba says. "It is his way." She runs in circles, chasing them, singing, "When in trouble, when in doubt, run in circles, scream and shout."

"Get out, Red and White! Time for you to play in the sunshine. Out!" she screams, aiming the longhaired broom at them to push them out. They don't want to go so they scurry around in circles in the hay. The white guinea pig takes the lead, followed by the red one, and finally the skinny black one, who clearly wants to sleep more.

Elena is bewildered as the circle game continues and Baba keeps screaming and shouting. "Up up up!" she scolds and then climbs onto the low bunk of the hutch. The guinea pigs follow. Bent at the waist, Baba wriggles the broom between her crooked legs. Then she pops up like toast and swings the broomstick at Elena, who ducks and touches Kukla, who brings calm, like a deep breath.

Baba's face twists into a scowl and drool dribbles from her mouth like when she's hungry. She stares at Elena's apron pocket. Elena knows she wants something from her. She squeezes Kukla—a protective instinct. *Maybe Baba is jealous and wants my doll*, she thinks. *Or maybe she wants me to show her my doll?*

"Take another broom; sweep up this mess," Baba says. "Time for you to give up that doll."

Baba has never once mentioned Kukla before, never even acknowledged that she knows about her.

Elena doesn't dare say a thing. She bites her tongue and begins sweeping hay near the hutch, uncovering the living space. The rhythmic swishing sounds of the broom barely calm the distress rising through her limbs. Baba has lied to her all these years. Rage toward the old woman fills her body. Burning with heat inside, she sweeps at a faster pace, anxious that Baba might resort to taking her doll from her.

"That's it—get this place clean," Baba directs. "I can't think with this mess. And stop your pouting."

Elena redirects her energy and sweeps the hay into the guinea hutch. When she's done, it's not perfect, but at least the space is orderly and civil again. She stops sweeping and turns to Baba.

"What do you want to ask?" Baba asks, smiling a gaping grin.

"Tell me about that strange woman," Elena says. "The cab driver and Father Al have met her. I know she was here. The cab driver says she's your sister. Can that be so, Baba Vera?"

"*The white one is my day, so light; the red one is my sun, so bright; and the black one is my darkest night.*" Baba sings this riddle by way of answering her.

"Shouldn't I know, Baba, if there is a wild woman looking for me?"

"You are so smart, my dear."

Red, White, and Black rush out from hiding, then settle at Baba Vera's crooked toes. She sits back on her hay bed where she naps, her legs outstretched. Elena can only imagine that this habit is a remnant from her past in some country village. Baba has never said.

"Now I am hungry, get my food," Baba commands. "Enough of this chit-chat." Then, in a softer voice, she says, "In good time, then. Those who know too much grow old too soon."

Elena scoops the last of the hay into neat piles and shovels it into the bed of the guinea pig hutch.

"My food!" Baba screams again. Her anger is rising. "And don't forget the cabbage." She licks her lips.

"Yes, Baba," Elena says. "I'll go pick the vegetables from the garden."

"That'll do for today, dear, but tomorrow I will eat duck."

"Can I get cooked duck at the market?"

"It must be a fresh duck," Baba says. "To cook, you must kill. Do it tonight on your way home and bring it back fresh for me tomorrow morning."

Hunting! Tonight! Elena cringes. She has never hunted, nor has she wanted to. Though she's carved fresh meats, she's never dreamed of killing. What in the world does Baba intend for her to do? *How will I ever manage to kill a duck?*

Elena shivers. Trembling, fumbling, she says, "Grandma, I have only carved meat as a butcher, cutting the tenders and flank steaks as you've taught me. I don't feel prepared for hunting." She stumbles in her excitement and grabs her doll, and just as she does the guineas rush in front of her, tripping her. Kukla dislodges from her hand and falls onto the floor. Like lightning, Baba is there, grabbing for her—but Elena recovers her to her pocket quickly.

"You won't need that doll anymore, Elena. You can leave her here with me. I'll care for her." Baba reaches out toward her apron pocket.

Elena instinctively steps back, clutching Kukla, not wanting to give her over. She's stunned, too, to hear Baba call her by her name, Elena.

A wide grin appears on Baba's face. She softens and begins to sing high-pitched sounds that remind Elena of a Gregorian chant she's heard sung at Our Lady. Like a chant, Baba's sounds are mysterious, joyful, and solemn at the same time. She sings a new song to Elena, unlike the zany riddles or the *fee, fi, fo, fums.* She's not screaming and shouting. This song has notes that reach toward the heavens, like the songs Father Al sings. Baba has a new expression on her face, one Elena has never witnessed. She looks beautiful, like she's a young woman.

Baba's eyes glaze over and a sweet smile graces her face, as if she has been transported to a nicer place; it takes away the shriveled, dried-apple look she usually carries. There is a moment of sweet silence between them. Elena feels loved and awash in Baba's radiant gaze. The haunted witch-child relationship melts for a moment. The broomstick is still. Baba no longer appears to have a heart of stone; she appears more divine, like Father Al's pictures of Blessed Mother Mary that hang in Our Lady.

"What have you seen, grandmother?" Elena finds it easy to call her "grandmother" and to ask her a question in this special moment.

"I recognize the ringlet of the doll's hair as my own," Baba says, sighing sweetly, a peaceful sigh rushing out.

Elena does not know how this can be. With her doll near her chest, she touches Kukla's hair, making a golden ring around her finger. Could it be that Baba sewed her own hair into Kukla when Elena was a baby? Could Baba be her real grandmother?

Then like thunder following lightning, Baba Vera becomes her familiar self. Her gnarled and wrinkled face is back and she begins twirling on her broom, raising dust and hell and getting the sleeping animals up and in a tizzy. "It must be a fresh duck, remember!" she yells. "Do it tonight on your way home. Tomorrow, a feast."

Elena has been previously disturbed by Baba's insatiable appetite for raw meat—hearts and tongues and gizzards; her dissonant, harsh commands for Elena to do this, sweep that, wash piles of inside-out clothes by hand; her play with Red, White, and Black, giving them the run of the house; and how can she appear so huge when in fact she's smaller than Elena? Now, Elena leaves the room feeling confused by everything—Baba's transformation, her saying Kukla's hair is her own, and this call for a duck. She's ordered Elena to do crazy things before, but nothing like this.

Elena goes outside toward the animals, fingering the soft ringlet of hair on Kukla's head. A lump of tears behind her eyes feels ready to burst like a thundercloud. Out of earshot, in the farthest corner of the forest-like garden in the back of the house, she kneels beside Piglet and prays for courage, emanating Father Al's prayers for grace. *What did she mean that Kukla's ringlet is her own? Is she really going to make me kill a duck? And what will be next?*

The pig nuzzles her face, sniffing near her eyes as if to pull out the tears falling into the mud. Piglet licks away her tears, then nibbles at Elena, demanding her walk.

This gesture is reassuring; Elena grabs the leash and takes Piglet around the garden, watching her sniff at everything. Today is the garden tour, Piglet's favorite, where she wets her nose tasting the veggies.

They stop and Elena kneels on the raised beds to survey the crops. The autumn harvest will yield the last tomatoes, zucchini, and heads of lettuce. She digs, remembering her task for today: veggie stew with cabbage. She pulls up potatoes and carrots and picks a head of cabbage, envisioning a savory stew with tarragon, sage, and parsley. The white plastic pail at the edge of the row fills like magic.

Before she enters the kitchen with the garden's gifts, Elena brings Piglet back to the hutch and fills her pen with some of the harvest.

"Thank you for your company," she says as she closes the hutch.

"Baba Vera," Elena calls, "I'm back with your lunch." She puts her pail near the sink and begins her prep, sorting, washing, and peeling the vegetables—especially the root vegetables, which cling to the deep earth they came from.

"Don't go rinsing off all of that dirt; that's where the minerals live!" Baba yells, making her jump.

"I'm learning so much from you, Grannie," Elena says automatically, trying to placate her. If she had her own druthers she would rinse and peel away the mineral contents from the root vegetables and save the peels for Koza the goat. Instead, under Baba's watchful gaze, she trims the tops from the carrots and puts the potatoes, beets, turnips, rutabagas—mineral dirt and all—into the five-gallon pot of boiling water on the iron stove.

The dirt melts away and the water turns a rich brown. The tomatoes, skin on, make a red sauce. Finally, she sprinkles in tarragon, parsley, chili peppers. Baba likes her stew red-hot and spicy. The five-gallon pot stews. Elena knows it will have to cook for three hours before it will be ready. When it's time, Baba will want to top it off with chicken livers and hearts.

Baba watches Elena complete her tasks with knowing eyes, the guinea pigs nestled on her lap now. "You are so smart," she says. "You must have good luck."

"Thank you," Elena says. She reflects the jobs that have been hers for the seven years she's been coming to Taraval Street: to tend to Baba's insatiable appetite, to cut and carve challenging cuts of meats, to watch and feed the fire under the kettle, to keep a garden and learn to let things grow and let things die. As she silently lists all these things, she realizes they're all means of survival. What is Baba preparing her for? Is she teaching her life's secrets, like when to allow and when to let go? Is she preparing her for some job outside this house?

The red guinea pig twirls around Elena, pulling her away from her reflections. Elena sees the small bits of light coming in from the window and how they reflect on the guineas' whiskers. *The sun*—yes, red is the hot morning sun that brings up light. Now she gets it. For Baba, each animal is a symbol for the rhythms of day and night. White is the sun of midday and black the night. Elena understands now. Then she wonders if Baba wanting her to let go of her doll has something to do with the cycles of day and night, as red, white, and black symbolize. Is she teaching Elena about things rising and falling like the sun in the sky? Is she lining her up for a transition within her own life cycle? No matter—Elena is certain she doesn't want to give up Kukla.

Soon the house fills with the sweet earth scents of the root vegetables, tarragon, and parsley. Baba begins to gurgle and salivate in anticipation of the tasty stew, the garden's fall bounty. She hops down to feed the guinea pigs the carrot tops, then fills an enormous metal bowl with scoops of the savory stew. Finally, she reaches into her apron pocket, pulls out the small heart and liver of a chicken, and pops them into her mouth. She chews ravenously, holding the bowl with her splayed thumbs and bony fingers, then slurps the soft stew. When she's done eating, she lies down in the hay bed next to her pets and falls asleep immediately. She snores so deeply the rafters shake.

While Baba sleeps, the three animals ride the waves of her tummy, expanding and contracting with each breath.

Elena cleans the pots and pans before taking her white cape and red sack from the middle room and walking into De-doo's shop, where he's fast asleep in his hand-built chair. She stares at the small, round man with his white mustache and beard, marveling at how hidden he manages to be in the little house on Taraval. She almost never hears him coming and going. She stands in front of the sleeping man and stares until he opens an eye.

She smiles and comes closer. "I am puzzled, dear Dedushka."

"Yes, dear, what is it?"

"It's Baba. Today I saw her change in front of my eyes."

"Tell me," he says.

She tells the story, starting with the doll dropping from her pocket, Baba claiming the blond ringlet on Kukla's head to be her own, and Baba then looking so beautiful and calm—singing, even.

He smiles and sits up in his chair, seeming alert and interested.

"Dedushka, am I dreaming all of this? Is it just me?"

"You've seen another dimension of her—love—that is all."

"And what if I can't kill a duck? And what if she takes Kukla away? I can't give her up."

"Elena, dear, you have a choice. Ask your inner guide to help you with these questions. You may continue to follow it."

"Who is Baba?" she prods.

"She is a magnificent being."

"And Dedushka, what about Anya? Is she here to reclaim me?"

"No, Elena, you will be safe."

This is all she can hope for from De-doo, and it's enough. She takes her leave and resolves to go to her spot in the park where her duck friends live.

CHAPTER 7: *Team Elena*

*A*fter the girl went on her way, Frank dashed into the vestibule of the old church and knocked on the door of the sanctuary.

He waited for the old priest to open the door, his hands clutching the flowered oilcloth bag, the green scarf sticking out like the jointed leg of a spider. More than anything, dropping these things off was an excuse to talk to the priest about what he had witnessed on Taraval. He hoped the girl knew he was on her side. In fact, Anya was beginning to remind him of Arachne, the mythological woman who turned into a spider in a story Fred had read to him as a child.

The story was about two women, a mortal and a goddess. The two old women on Taraval reminded him of them. The similarities were disturbing. When Arachne challenged the goddess Athena to a weaving contest, Athena beat her over the head three times with her shuttle, then turned her into a spider. Had Anya challenged the other woman? Maybe she'd beat her on the head too and change her into a spider. He wondered how in the world he'd fallen into this web of alternate reality.

Footsteps. The knob turned. Frank came back to the moment.

"Hello, young man," the long-bearded priest said. "Come in." He remembered Frank.

Frank looked around, still clutching the damned bag, fearing the woman might pop up at any moment. She was unpredictable. Slippery.

The priest ushered him toward his private room behind the altar, the place where Frank had heard him speaking with Anya. He gestured to a chair. "Sit down," he said, then took a seat in the chair facing it.

Frank obeyed. "I took Anya to a house on Taraval yesterday," he said. He looked at the man sitting across from him.

"Go on," the priest said. His long beard stretched all the way down to his navel.

"Strange goings on in there."

"I can't imagine those two together after all these years."

"Who are they?"

"The girl's godparents."

"How can that be?" Frank asked. "They're like my wacky neighbor who howled at the full moon. We called her Doozie."

"Anya's the doozie. Vera and Victor are trustworthy."

Frank nodded. He didn't want to overstep, but he also appreciated having Anya's strangeness acknowledged. Then he told the priest what he had heard and seen, and how he'd overheard the other woman—Vera—say Anya had killed the girl's mother. When he was done, he asked, "Is any of this true?"

"Old business." The man pulled on his beard and offered nothing more.

"Who is Anya?" Frank asked. "She says the other one, Vera, is her sister."

"Of sorts."

"Vera said something about Anya putting a curse on the girl's mother," Frank said.

The priest nodded.

"The strangest thing, Father, is that I feel a fierce need to protect the girl, and I don't even know her name."

"Elena." The priest nodded again, which Frank felt was an indication of his approval.

"Who is Anya?"

"The evil twin. From an unfortunate realm. Spits like a camel."

"Yes, I'd say." Frank wrinkled his nose. "She spit at you on that first day, right before she got into the cab."

"Those two, in a spitting contest—I can see it." The priest laughed.

Frank was not so casual about what he'd experienced. How had he gotten mixed up in this mess? Again it felt like some fairy tale that should take place in a faraway land. Was this mere coincidence, or some kind of fate he'd fallen into? It certainly felt like a fateful day—like space out of time, kind of surreal. How could he pull away when he had this deep desire to protect the girl?

"Tell me what you saw," the priest said.

Frank walked him through what had happened—how he'd knocked on the door, urgently needing to use the bathroom, and how Victor had let him in. How through the walls he'd heard the two women arguing over Elena. How Vera had said she'd kill Anya if she tried to take Elena . . . that over her dead body would she let Anya harm her. He told the priest how his curiosity got the best of him and how he'd inched his way to an open door, and through it he'd seen the two of them spitting and hissing at each other, grabbing one another around the waist. How Anya had kicked a black animal—maybe a guinea pig or a rabbit—and how it had seemed as if one of the women, he couldn't see which one, had gone up in smoke, like a ghost.

"A ghost!" the priest repeated, his face more animated than Frank had seen it so far. Clearly, this revelation took the old man by surprise.

After a long silence, during which Frank had no idea what to say or do, the priest finally looked at him and said, "She's in good hands."

"Whose hands?"

"Mine and Vera and Victor's," he said. "And now yours."

"But—"

"And Elena has good sense, a kind of intuition that guides her." The priest got up and reached a hand out toward Frank. "Did you want to leave that bag with me?"

Frank handed over Anya's oilcloth bag and her printed scarf. "Yes, she left this on the passenger seat."

He smiled and put the bag on the table. "Thank you. She won't be needing these anymore."

Frank left the vestibule feeling somewhat assured. Elena had a team of people looking out for her. He wasn't sure he agreed with the priest that Vera and Victor were trustworthy, but the priest himself was trustworthy. And he felt the good Father had given his blessing for Frank to be part of Elena's team. Team Elena. The priest had knighted him as one of Elena's protectors.

He got back in the cab, relieved to be free of the woman's possessions. He checked in with his dispatcher and learned there was a passenger nearby waiting for a pickup. Going to work for a few hours would clear his head.

CHAPTER 8: *Elena's Blood Ritual*

With the sun low, Elena walks toward Golden Gate Park. Fear grips her, tightening around her body in bands of black, as the thought of killing the little duck takes hold. She walks toward the pond in Golden Gate Park as dusk, like a shade coming down on the day, greets her with a smile.

She sits on the edge of the pond, watching the ducks as they bathe and hunt for little worms and slugs, slimy leaves and grasses, before bedtime.

"Please help me, Kukla, please."

She feeds the nearby ducks bread from her hand, but it feels different this time, like she's sitting on the edge of the pond as a predator and not a friend. When the last duck, the littlest one, nears her outstretched hand, she grabs it around the breast. The duck stills. With one hand on its tummy and the other on its back, she cradles its body. She feels its rapid heartbeat. *Will my hands know what to do?* Although she's worked with meats, she's never killed a creature, especially one she loves. *Why must I do this, dear Kukla?*

She remembers De-doo's words—that she has a choice, that she has an inner guide about these questions. "You may continue to follow it," he'd said.

But Baba told her, "To cook, you must kill." *Is this a sacrifice I'm making?* she wonders. *For Baba Vera? Or for someone or something else?*

The duck nestles in closer to Elena's chest. She feels its heartbeat as if it is her own. The pulse of the bird, its rapid heartbeat, calms her. The animal seems as if it is willingly giving itself to her. She senses the duck is part of a ritual that she knows deep inside but doesn't totally understand. Baba has asked her to make a symbolic offering of something she loves. This is part of her training. But to what end? She does not know.

Her fingers find the duck's neck—so slender and smooth, with so many tiny bones entwined with one another, like a little puzzle. She meditates on its interlacing bones and closes her eyes. She twists with less effort than she imagined and the duck falls, as if asleep, into her lap. When Elena opens her eyes, the duck is lying there—quiet, dead still. It has no pulse. Elena pets it one last time, then picks it up by its feet and places it into her red sack, getting ready to leave.

As soon as she turns, she sees the cab driver maybe twenty feet from her, standing near bushes as tall as him. Is he hiding? Intentionally watching her? His posture is alert, like he's been caught doing something he shouldn't. *Here he is again*—she's too preoccupied to wonder why. He has witnessed what she's done. He doesn't move.

She turns toward his stunned eyes and sees a fiery red color—the reflection of the setting sun, she imagines. When she walks toward him it's like walking through a dream that he's a part of.

She stops and faces him. He raises his taut eyebrows and his eyes wander away from hers.

"You saw me kill the duck," she says, looking toward the water's edge where the duck took its last breath.

His eyes blink. His mouth falls open as if to speak. She automatically reaches a hand toward him, and he takes it.

Am I in his dream or is he in mine? It seems the two of them are related in this mystery that she doesn't understand.

She picks up on the man's fear. He seems astonished by her action. Her heart feels heavy, but his beats as rapidly as the duck's did right before the end. She wonders if he knows her dread in having completed this act. But the duck's passing from life to death has instilled in her a feeling of awe and respect for the life force. She feels like she's holding two sides of the world—complete yet spinning.

"Are you alright?" she finally asks.

He nods.

They walk toward the pond with the night falling, covered by the magic of colors of blue and red fire setting into the vast ocean, cooling her off. She pulls her cape tight around her neck. They talk for a while—then they release one another's hand and part.

She watches him until he disappears into the darkness.

Elena makes her way out of the park toward the church, patting the bird inside her bag, which she's slung diagonally across her chest—a front pack. As she walks home she ponders how it is that Frank was there in just the moment when the bird's life and spirit parted. She wonders where its spirit is now. She walks faster, eager to get to Father Al. She knows he will help her to make sense of this act, bring clarity to what she has done. In the meantime, the two-mile walk home settles her into a rhythm she knows well.

Coming out of the park, her eyes adjust to passing vehicles with their headlights shining. She waits for the pedestrian signal to cross Fulton, resting before the final five-block walk, mostly uphill, to her home.

When she arrives, she lets herself into a quiet vestibule. When she opens the door to the back of the inner chapel, the mosaic half-portrait of Jesus, reflecting light, looks as if he, too, holds a sacrifice in his hands.

She walks down the side aisle and opens the door into the kitchen, where she removes the duck from her red sack and places it on the table.

Father Al enters the room from the door on the opposite side of the kitchen and approaches her. He looks at the duck, and then at Elena. He reaches his hand out to her.

"Tell me about the duck, child," he says.

She takes his hand in hers. "Baba asked me to kill a duck and bring it to her tomorrow." She reaches over and touches the downy feathers of the dead bird. "Please help me to understand my actions."

"I always wondered what she would ask you to do." He looks at her with his compassionate eyes. "I too had a test I had to overcome."

"What was it, Father?"

"A Vision Quest. Do you know what that is?"

"No."

"It's a rite of passage to usher a young man into adulthood. I was sixteen."

She waits for him to say more.

"She wanted me to find my true nature in Nature, as she's asked you to do today. But I didn't like spending time at the ponds in the dark. I liked to read about Ulysses and other heroes on their journeys, to read sacred texts, reflective and symbolic teachings." He spreads his hands. "And there I was, spending the night alone. I was scared of all the sounds in the dell. But she was preparing me for my ministry by helping me see that I could be alone with discomfort—could sit through the night with animals scurrying about and not run away. When a coyote howled off in the distance, it was all I could do to stay there. I planned a hike up a tree should one appear." He laughs, shaking his head. "She wanted me to come through the night in one piece. She figured when I could handle my own discomfort, then I could be present for others, and come through any challenge whole."

Elena remembers him walking with her as a child in the park, pointing out all the plants and tiny creatures. He too learned to understand Nature because of Baba.

"Father, what kind of a ritual is Baba Vera making for me?"

"She is asking you to sacrifice something you love from the natural world. Being a huntress is part of your training."

He has validated her belief.

"I loved this duck, and I have killed it, Father."

"You had respect for this life." He touches the bird's feathers. His long fingers line up next to hers on the duck's back.

She nods. "Yes, I loved this little duck. She ate out of my hand and trusted me. I've betrayed her."

"We must make sacrifices in life in order to live," he says. "You are a young woman now, gifted, and will be challenged by new opportunities. I hope I can help you make sense of these things." He pulls out a handkerchief from his cassock. "As long as you honor the life of this bird, you have not betrayed it."

He offers her his handkerchief; she takes it and blows her nose, then looks into his eyes.

"Baba has asked you to descend, to draw on your instincts so you can pass from innocence into maturity and strengthen your calling, your purpose." He moves beside her and begins a prayer for the sacrifice of this innocent spirit being. He chants in Russian, words he must have learned as a boy. His sounds emanate from a deep source within him. To Elena's ears, it sounds like a choir of voices all coming from different parts of the small church and meeting at a center point. She feels alive and grateful for Father Al's blessings. She shivers as he prays.

When he finishes his prayers, his gaze meets hers.

"Thank you for blessing us, dear Father," she says.

He nods and leaves the kitchen through the far door for his private sanctuary, closing the door behind him. She imagines the candles he will light, shimmering like a morning sun bringing up a new day.

She gathers up the duck in both her hands, pondering her act and the man who witnessed it once again. Consoled by Father Al's words, she accepts her action as being in the service of her calling and the next stage of life. She hears Father Al chanting in the small room behind the door from the kitchen. She automatically puts her hand in her pocket, feeling for her doll, and is grateful for her guidance too. She feels safe knowing that both Father Al and Kukla will protect and nourish her through this sacred rite of passage.

She readies herself to package the duck that she will bring to Baba for tomorrow's lunch. She wraps it in white paper, creasing the ends, and places it in the cold storage. She will prepare the meat tomorrow at Baba Vera's.

Father Al reminded her that she is a young woman now. She knows this to be true by the way blood stains the white pads she now has to wear once a month.

CHAPTER 9: *Frank as Witness*

After the talk with the priest, Frank picked up some fares in the neighborhood, then stopped at home for a snack. Dusk now, and his worrying mind landed on the girl's—Elena's—safety. He knew she would soon be cutting through the park on her way home. He jumped up and gathered his keys. He left his apartment and drove into the park with the idea to run interference should that crazy woman show up.

He went over his plans. He'd park a little distance from the pond and find a spot where she wouldn't see him. He didn't want to startle her, only to know her whereabouts and to prevent a kidnapping. He was sure that if Anya were to encounter Elena, she would snatch her right up. Ever since seeing that woman spitting and kicking and hissing her threats, he'd felt compelled to protect Elena from her. And Father Al had given him his blessing, hadn't he?

Frank pulled up near the pond where he'd last seen her, parked his car a distance from the water's edge, removed his shoes, and walked softly through the grass. As he approached, he made out a small figure in white, sitting in silence. He hid in a bush nearby and peered out toward the water.

Her hair reflected strawberry light from the setting sun. She was kneeling, bending over the water's edge. Her hand reached toward a gaggle of ducks, feeding them like the last time. Then he saw the last one—a small one, the runt—come close for its food. The duck was eating out of her hand when she swiftly and suddenly caught its body in her two hands. She put one hand around its stomach and the other behind its head. And then he heard it—*snap!*

He gasped, but she somehow didn't hear him.

She sat a moment longer, then put the duck in her bag and rose to leave. As she did, she turned her head and saw him. She looked surprised—and then not. She just looked at him, her eyes reflecting for him his own frightened face, as if holding up a mirror to him so he could see his reflection.

She walked toward him until she was just a few feet away from where he stood planted.

He froze.

He looked away from her, listening to the pond for any sounds that might indicate the runty duck was missed. But it was quiet—as if this was supposed to be, or as if it never happened. In the spell of the girl, he hadn't heard their uproar or any attempt by the ducks to snap at her. Now a sickening thought flooded his mind. What if Anya had something to do with this act?

"You saw me kill the duck," she said, looking back at the pond.

She was standing in front of him, the red sack hanging on her shoulder and across her chest. His heart pounded. She seemed to see through him to his pain. She waited and watched, and then reached out a hand to him. He took it.

"Are you alright?" she asked.

He nodded. Hand in hand, they walked to the water's edge.

"I must have had a panic attack," he said when he finally gained his bearings. His mind was flooded with thoughts as he tried to rationalize this sudden surge of adrenaline—his own loss of his mother as a child, and also those two wicked sisters. He knew what Elena had just done was connected to them, likely mandated by them—but what could he say? He looked down at his feet.

"Where are your shoes?" she asked.

"In the cab. I was trying to be quiet. I didn't want you to think I was stalking you." He smiled. "Not such a good job, huh?"

"Is that what you were doing?"

"Well, not exactly. I just wanted to make sure that you were safe."

"Safe?"

"From that woman—Anya. She thinks she's your mother."

"Thank you for saying that. Father Al only told me the woman who visited him was misdirected."

Frank snorted. "I'd say she's crazy."

Elena nodded. "Besides, my mother would not scream at Father Al the way she did."

"You heard her scream?"

"Yes, I was there when she visited the church."

Frank felt even more uneasy now, thinking that Anya might go back to the church and grab Elena there. He envisioned all sorts of methods she'd use to get her. He shook with fear.

"Are you alright to drive home?" Elena asked.

He took a deep breath, nodded, and managed a smile, but it felt tense and twisted.

"I must be on my way now. Father Al will be waiting for me."

They let go of one another's hands, and Elena turned on her heel and walked away from him.

Frank walked to his cab, opened the door, and got in. He watched as Elena turned and crossed Middle Drive toward her home. He envied her litheness; how she knew the ways of the forest; how easily and carefully she'd killed the duck. He had never encountered anyone like her before, and the thought occurred to him that she was almost of another era, or of another world; that she may not need his protection; that he had been presumptuous; that she was braver than he. Yet he knew Anya was out to get her, and he was determined to be there for Elena.

Then he imagined her working in his brother's kitchen, as she was so comfortable with meat. He didn't know where this thought came from. But she *was* a huntress. He had once gone duck hunting with his dad, but the only thing he'd liked about it was the curious ways of the ducks, especially how they landed with their feet skimming the water and then just plopped down. Unlike Elena, he hadn't made a kill. In fact, he couldn't. And he'd never wanted to work in the kitchen with Fred, either. He didn't even like to eat wild game.

The girl's name was Elena, not Vasilisa. Why had Anya called her that? Perhaps that was her given name, though he doubted the woman could be this girl's mother. It reassured him that Elena too doubted Anya was her mother.

What was he falling into with this strange cast of characters? An alternate reality? A strangeness he couldn't name, certainly. And still the nagging question: *Is she safe with those wackos?* He thought about the two sisters and the hissing and spitting, the fighting, the smoke that seemed like voodoo. Had he really seen that, or was it his imagination? Father Al had seemed to believe it. It occurred to him that maybe he was in a magical spell. How could he know?

He needed a good night's sleep, and then a chat with Jane, the evolutionary biologist from Mill Valley he'd picked up at SFO a few weeks earlier. She'd asked him to stop at Ocean Beach; they'd spent a breezy hour together searching for snowy plovers, an endangered species.

He'd felt carefree with her. She'd been so reassuring. "Things are as they're supposed to be," she'd said. "Isn't the imprint already within the caterpillar before the butterfly?"

After their day together she'd invited him to a lecture at Dominican College, where she'd spoken about imaginal cells. He'd been riveted. She had given him her card. Maybe she could help.

The next day, after leaving Henry O in the financial district, Frank swore he saw Elena disappear into the coffee crowd around a stand. But he quickly realized his imagination was playing tricks on him, that she really wasn't in the crowd. She was a strong presence for him, however. It reminded him of his experience after losing his mother. He'd seen her everywhere. Now, as then, it comforted him. In this case it gave him the illusion that Elena was safe.

He sat a minute longer with his thoughts, wondering again what Jane would call it. She'd surely have a name for it.

He resolved to call Jane today, or maybe even go find her. But first he needed caffeine.

He parked his cab in the green zone and grabbed a coffee at the cart. He got back in his cab and sipped the dark coffee, taking time to people watch. He turned to his right to see Henry O's face poking through the open passenger window.

"You're still here! My lucky day," Henry said. "The boss is away."

"You got your wish," Frank said.

"Yeah! I'm contemplating my day. Looks like you are too."

Frank nodded.

Henry glanced back at the cart. "Hold on, let me get a coffee."

Soon Henry was sitting in the passenger seat next to Frank with a steaming cup in his hands. "What's up, kid?"

"Thinking about a weird woman," he said. "Claims she has a daughter in San Francisco, but something's funny."

"Do you believe her?"

Frank shook his head. "She's lying. And I can't stop thinking 'bout the girl she claims is her daughter."

"So what's the deal? You in love?"

"No, man, the girl can't be more than fifteen. And she looks twelve. I feel like I'm supposed to protect her."

"Is she in danger?"

"Maybe. And she's different—the way she acts, the way she dresses. She wears a weird outfit, a white cape and a ribbon in her hair."

"Sounds like Little Red Riding Hood," Henry said. He took a sip of coffee.

"Exactly, she was in danger too. The big bad wolf."

"Yeah, who disguised himself as a grandmother."

"There's a grandmother in this story too." Frank again felt that unreal quality of the situation. "And these women are as witchy as any real witches."

He told Henry about the trip to Taraval and the eccentric sisters, how they tripped him out. He told him about the duck.

"Haven't heard of anyone doing that before," Henry said.

"Yeah, weird. She's like a . . . huntress or something."

"In Golden Gate Park in 2020!" Henry shook his head in wonder. "You got caught up in something strange, kid. You ought to be careful." He looked at Frank with tenderness.

"What the hell's going on?" Frank wondered aloud, and he realized he was speaking about two things—the entirety of Elena's situation, but also his own involvement in something no one had asked him to meddle with. And yet he knew he was in too deep. He would not be walking away.

Henry O nudged him. "Take it easy, buddy. It's gonna be okay."

"Thank you. You're right. The whole thing is just so strange," Frank marveled.

As they sat together in front of the coffee cart these questions circled in Frank's mind, reminding him of all the times he'd asked Fred about the deaths of their beloved parents—what had happened, and why. The same confusions gripped him now as he sat amidst the skyscrapers, the coffee drinkers, and the mass of people walking by the cab. Maybe he was hallucinating, like when his parents died and he was seeing his mom everywhere. Yes, what he was experiencing now felt strange yet similar to the day they buried them. They were at the cemetery in San Bruno, and Frank was convinced his mother was not in the metal casket at all—that she had escaped.

"Fred, Fred, look, look up." Frank had pointed to a low-flying red-tailed hawk. "Do you see her?" He knew the hawk flying so low above his head had something to do with his mother's spirit.

"I see her, buddy," Fred had said, holding his hand.

Later, he'd told Frank the experience was more than a hallucination.

"This is a common occurrence, some kind of a sensitive intuition," Fred had said. "It sure is extraordinary. Sensing our loved ones like you did helps us to grieve. I see Mom and Dad, too."

Frank leaned into his intuition now. Knowing not to trust Anya was perhaps what allowed him to feel a part of this club that hadn't invited him in. He and Father Al were part of a team to protect Elena—he was sure of it. He could trust this feeling. He breathed in this thought, aware that he'd been holding his breath.

When he looked up, Henry O was still there, looking tenderly at him.

"Thank you for listening," Frank said.

"You good?"

"I'm good. See you at five."

Henry put a hand on Frank's shoulder and then got out. Frank shook his head, not sure of any of it. He finished his coffee and checked in with his dispatcher.

"Where the hell were you, Frank? GPS looks like you're sitting your lazy fat ass somewhere on Market Street, maybe in a yellow or red zone," the dispatcher said.

Frank touched his skinny ass. "It hasn't grown, has it?" he said back through the receiver, laughing. He was grateful his work depended on his own initiative and not the cab company. He owned the car, Fred's gift to him. Could leave the company any time. Become an Uber driver. He chuckled at the way things were changing.

Frank drove up Geary; when he passed the George, he kept an eye out for Anya. He was grateful when he didn't see her there, but also keenly aware that her absence didn't mean the threat to Elena was any less real.

He pushed the pedal down and drove off.

CHAPTER 10: *The Heart of the Duck*

When Elena arrives today at Baba Vera and Dedushka Victor's, she makes her way through the workshop with the duck. De-doo's nowhere to be seen. Neither is Baba; there are no *fee, fi, fo, fums* today.

She hangs her cape and carries the red sack through the sitting room. Her head tall, she enters the kitchen and sees Baba perched on the upper bunk of the hutch.

"You're here; it's about time," Baba says. She straddles the edge of the hay mattress, her skirt above her bony knees, her spindly legs kicking back and forth, her bare toes—long, like fingers—curling and uncurling.

Her claw-like nails aid her in climbing down the beam that separates the lower bunk from the upper. She jumps down and rushes toward Elena, seemingly eager to see what she carries in her bag.

"I have the duck for you, Grandma," Elena says, not startled by Baba's antics.

"Where?" Baba grabs for the cloth bag.

Elena takes a step back, then removes the duck, swaddled in white paper, from her red sack. She holds it out to Baba, who snatches it eagerly.

"You are a good daughter to me," she says. She takes the duck to the table, where she unwraps and examines it, poking her skinny fingers into its eyes and mouth, touching its feet, smoothing her fingers over its webbed toes. "And the gizzard and the tongue?"

"Yes, for the sauté."

"I love duck feet," she says, looking into Elena's eyes.

"Yes, you will have the feet to munch and all the organs in your stew," Elena says, standing beside her. "Now rest."

Baba returns to the lower bunk of the hutch and watches her through softer, almost calm, eyes. Elena knows Baba recognizes her competence in having completed this task, that she is satisfied with her skills enough to rest.

Elena sets to work: She places the duck on the butcher table and then gathers her tools—a sharp knife she'll use to remove the beautiful downy breast and poultry scissors to cut off the head and then the feet. The wings come next. She knows so clearly what to do. Now that the duck's spirit is free, Elena is once again a skilled butcher. She marvels at the large wingspread compared to the small drumsticks. Baba loves these thighs, with their sweetness and tender flesh. Elena slips the knife under the skin and makes a slice up the duck's center, removing the skin just the way Baba taught her. Then she pulls feathers off its breast, placing her small hands under its skin, slipping off the beautiful feather garment from the animal's muscular red body. The breast, now exposed, shines brightly, reflecting the light of the kitchen candle.

She easily removes the gizzards, heart, and liver. Baba loves these parts too. Maybe they will go into a stew, but Baba has also been known to eat them raw. Elena thinks of what Baba said yesterday: "To cook, you must kill." For sure this is the point she's making for Elena with this test. Elena now has the recognition, as never before, that the meat she eats has been sacrificed for her nourishment. She gets it. Through Baba's tests, she learns and integrates in her own way.

She works steadily, preparing the duck with love and gratitude for the skills Baba has taught her, and for Kukla, who gives her protection. Today she has hidden Kukla in her underskirt pocket. Baba's grab for her doll yesterday put Elena on edge, despite her understanding that much of Baba's behavior is in service of her training. Father Al has confirmed as much.

Elena finishes carving the sections. "Close your eyes and open your mouth," she says, turning away from the butcher table. She walks toward the hay bed, from which Baba has been watching this whole time. Baba gets up and meets Elena halfway between the bed and the table.

"Don't tease me."

"Slowly, please, Baba. I have something for you."

Baba moves closer to Elena. Her face becomes child-like. She sucks at her teeth before opening her mouth. She does not close her eyes, and Elena doesn't press the issue. She places the small duck heart into Baba's mouth and watches the old woman suck the bite-size heart, humming and slurping, before she chews.

"Oh, yes, and these are for the stew." Elena points toward the entrails, where the gizzard, liver, and tongue rest. She walks to the pot on the stove and drops the inner organs of the duck into the boiling water, keeping out the gizzard and tiny tongue to sauté.

Baba looks pleased; she jumps onto the lower bunk of the hutch and leans her head back. Red and White scatter and run toward the warmth of the stove. Only the black guinea pig stays behind.

"Sleep now, the stew will be ready after your nap," Elena says as she tucks a blanket over Baba's toes, which have straw hanging out between them. Baba loves her afternoon nap.

Elena cleans and wraps what remains of the entrails in the white paper for the compost. She sweeps and begins to make order of the untidy room, hoping the swishing sounds of the straw will lull Baba to sleep, even though she wants to hear more about the woman, Anya—to ask if Baba is really her sister and Anya is really Elena's mother.

But now her reticence in asking seems to wane and her intuition tells her to speak. She notices how she holds on to an unspoken agreement not to ask. Where did that come from? Was it her own shyness? Baba's teaching? She remembers that Kukla used to encourage her not to ask certain questions, and as she got older she agreed certain questions should not be asked. Or, put another way, some questions were unanswerable. She remembers asking Father Al, *What are people? Why are we here? Where would we be if the world was not here? What is the earth?*

"Dear child, we'll be talking about these things for a long time," he answered.

Since then, so many of her questions have remained unanswered—like, does the red guinea pull up the sun? Or do the brooms Baba uses to run in circles hold magic? Or are the skulls related to Baba and De-doo? Elena has let many of these questions pass by like clouds on a windy day. But now she begins to understand discernment and feels a possible opening in this defense.

As she ponders all this, she rubs herbs on the duck breasts, thighs, and wings and fries the meat on a high heat for a scrumptious meal. Then she deglazes the pan, sautés the gizzard and the tongue, and adds the carrots, onions, potatoes, beets, and a few leftover cherry tomatoes from the summer garden. She pours in some stock from the boiling pot and finally the cabbage and lets it all sit together. The scent wraps itself around the room, savory and delicious.

Baba inhales deeply and sits up. "That woman doesn't belong here," she says. "She will soon disappear."

Elena drops the chopping knife and quickly bends to pick it up. The guineas scatter away from the back of the burner, where they've been munching on the veggie scraps. They scurry to the hutch and jump inside the lower bunk, landing on Baba's long toes, and proceed to rub her feet with their noses in the way Elena rubbed the duck with the spices. Baba has always seemed to have a wiretap on her thoughts, which makes her nervous. Perhaps that, too, has contributed to her reticence to speak.

The scent of cabbage lifts above the others and pulls her away from her thoughts. The stink irritates her nose, makes the little hairs inside scream. Cabbage, the staple of Russian food, doesn't appeal to her. It's a wet, dark smell whose leftover trace lingers—not unlike the woman who has infiltrated her life in these past days.

"Ask me," Baba says. "I know you want to ask."

"Is that woman my mother?" Elena asks, emboldened by Baba's demand, suddenly feeling that she can push more directly than is her usual custom.

Baba sighs a deep breath out.

"Is she?" Elena presses.

"She is *not* your mother," Baba snaps. "She is evil. She is what happens to you when you are jealous, when you have envy, when you are consumed by hatred and greed. It is our task to banish her."

Elena trembles at Baba's soliloquy, yet her insides relax too, reassured that the woman is not her mother and will soon disappear. She feels excited, too, seeing how her anger helped her to ask the question.

She once again recalls Father Al's words about the screaming woman. He said she was "misdirected." Then she remembers his story about how he found Elena in the church as a baby with her little doll pinned to her white blanket and a note from her mother attached.

Dear Elena, The Wise, The Beautiful, The Fair,

I feel so much sorrow to leave you here, but I feel joy as well because I know you will be safe with Father Al. He is a good person who has helped me here in San Francisco.

While I must return to Russia, I leave you this little doll with my blessing. Keep her with you always. If you are ever in trouble, give the doll something to eat and ask its advice. She will show you the way.

With love,

Masha, your mother

Elena repeats her mother's words from the note she long ago memorized. It's tucked into her favorite fairy tale book. She squeezes Kukla as she repeats in her mind, *I leave you this little doll with my blessing. Keep her with you always.*

Elena knows these could not be the words of Anya. She is sure now that her Baba Vera will use fire energy to banish that ugly woman. She is certain that Baba has given her the gift of providing her with all the tools she needs to live in the world. Perhaps this, too, is a kind of fire.

Elena cries tears of joy at her redemption, like she's gaining a sense of herself, and this makes her happy.

"Why are you crying?" Baba asks.

"It's just the onions," Elena lies.

"Now go, get out of here," Baba scolds her. "There's no room for tears here." But as she says this, she smiles.

CHAPTER 11: *The Moleskin Pouch*

*A*fter driving past the George, Frank took a right on Van Ness, toward Fisherman's Wharf. Scanning the crowd where tourists and commuters at the ferry building rushed from their ferries, he saw a potential passenger waving: a middle-aged man, dapper, wearing a bowler hat, standing at the curb.

Frank stopped and the gentleman got in.

"The Geary Theatre, please," the man said. He proceeded to tell Frank he was an actor and would be rehearsing his role as Cornelius Fudge, the Minister of Magic, in *Harry Potter.*

Frank looked into his rearview mirror, thinking the guy was putting him on. Cornelius, in character in the back seat, played with a little music box he held in his hand and entertained Frank with stories of wizardry and songs for the next handful of blocks.

"A musical," he said as they pulled up to the theatre. He paid and gave Frank a moleskin pouch he pulled from a great pocket, said it was to hold his favorite talisman. "A magic token for your assistance," he said, "a protection."

Frank took the rich brown purse—it felt like mink—and thanked him. The man let himself out, tipped his bowler hat, bowed, and turned toward the side door of the theatre.

Weird, Frank thought, examining the soft, furry purse, pulling the drawstrings to see inside, hoping some clue to his dilemma hid there. Perhaps Cornelius had left a talisman for him. His fingers found nothing, but the pouch seemed to expand to accommodate his search. He put the purse in the glove compartment.

He took this meeting as a sign to take the rest of the day off. It was a little too crazy, which mirrored his life of late. Everything was a little too crazy. His head was spinning.

It was still early, near 9:00 a.m.; just an hour had passed since he'd first gotten Henry O to work. He continued west toward home. He passed the George once again—that made two times today; he was compelled, it seemed, like a moth to the flame—then made his way to Pine, a fast one-way street that ran parallel to Sacramento, the street where his brother Fred worked as a chef.

A block from Fred's bistro he turned, then turned again onto Sacramento and parked, readying himself to go in to talk with Fred about the witches. He laughed at the absurdity of his last few days. He listened to his stomach churn, telling him how nervous he was, how ashamed he was to tell Fred about his fears. In an anxiety cloud, he sat still, watching early-morning pedestrians walk with their cell phones toward coffee shops.

When his stomach settled, he got out of his cab, entered the restaurant, and walked through the main dining room toward the kitchen. He peeked in to find the staff prepping vegetables and meats. Fred stood half-bent over the stockpot, smelling the concoction inside. Frank knew his brother relied on smell to determine what the broth still needed. He had a good nose, especially for wine.

Fred finished, turned toward the door, and made eye contact.

"What are you doing here, Frank, everything okay?"

"You have a minute?"

"I do; in fact, I was looking for an excuse to breakfast at our favorite Russian bakery."

"Cinderella?" Frank couldn't believe he was inviting him to join.

"Let's play hooky, have a morning Napoleon, maybe a soup," Fred said.

"It's barely nine."

"You drive," Fred said. "I've been here since six, I need a break."

Fifteen minutes later, Frank pulled up at the Cinderella Bakery and Café on Balboa. They ordered inside and sat at an outside table with their lattes and Napoleons, the layered cream puffs, their tradition. Frank had a sweet tooth and this was the place where he could indulge it. Fred usually denied his sweet tooth but today he ordered one as well.

"So what's up?" Fred asked, wiping his hands on his napkin.

"I met a young girl, Elena," Frank said. "I'm worried about her. She's fifteen, looks younger. Wears a white cape. I spotted her hanging around the taxi while I was waiting for a passenger one day." He took a huge bite of his cream puff.

"Unusual outfit for a teenager in San Francisco."

"Yeah, she's unusual for a teenager."

"Did she say what she wanted?"

"No, we didn't speak then. I had never seen the girl before." Frank sipped his latte. "But now I'm convinced she's in danger." He wanted to say that he felt like he was getting in over his head and maybe even that he was in danger of being swallowed up into her world, their world. He wanted to slow it down. But how to explain all that?

"In danger of being kidnapped," he elaborated. "And harmed. I want to protect her, but I barely know her."

"You want to save her," Fred said as the waiter came with their soups.

"Yeah." Frank moved his cream puff to make room for the *pelmeni*—dumplings stuffed with cheese in a chicken broth for him and Babushka's chicken soup for Fred.

"Remember Ma's chicken soup?" his brother asked, his nose almost touching the broth. "It was just like this."

"Ma's eclairs," Frank said. "That's what I remember."

"She was a great pastry chef. Maybe that's why you eat your cream puff before the main," Fred teased. He pointed toward Frank's enormous cream pastry, already half-gone.

Frank looked away, choking down that feeling rising upwards through his sinuses and stinging his eyes. The stream could so easily spill over on the downhill and bring tears. Afraid to remember, afraid to show Fred his tears, he cleared his throat and cuffed his brother on the arm.

"Just love the Napoleons, that's all," he managed to say. "The woman I was waiting for when I first saw the girl," he said, turning the conversation back toward Elena, "she claims to be the girl's mother. I believed her at first, but then . . . then everything got a little weird. When I took her to see her sister on Taraval Street, I saw them get into a wicked fight, with spitting and cursing." He paused for a moment, deciding not to tell his brother how one of them vanished into thin air. "But mostly I feel confused, like I'm part of this story. It's a little unreal, like when I was seeing Mama everywhere."

Fred sat up. "Why are you so involved?"

"I keep bumping into the girl, at the park, and I'm seeing her in other places too—places where I know she isn't. It's like it's fate."

"You've got to let go of the girl," Fred said.

"That's not so easy to do. She's on my mind." Frank didn't tell his brother how the dissolving witch and the other stuff was on his mind too. He couldn't, not yet. He had to wrestle with it himself a bit longer.

"You've got good control, buddy," Fred said.

Frank dropped his spoon, and as he fumbled to recover it, he didn't feel sure he was good at anything these days. He looked at Fred. "What do you mean?"

"You stopped drinking and have a steady job."

Frank gave him a skeptical look.

"Drop this business with the girl," Fred said again. "That's a good place to start."

Frank didn't know if anything could get him to drop it; the girl and her strange pursuer had gotten under his skin. Nonetheless, he felt grateful for Fred's compliment. It let a little light crack through his dismal mood.

After their impromptu brunch, Frank drove his brother back to the bistro, then drove toward home. The fog in the outer Richmond was like gray velvet; it matched his mood. He passed a clump of stores on the Avenues, sprinkled amongst the Russian onion domes. He loved these domes of turquoise, cobalt, and golden hues.

The Russians who had migrated to the north coast of California in the early 1800s and become involved with the sea, hunting otters for the fur trade, had designed these domes. After the mammals disappeared and the fur trade diminished, the community had stayed in San Francisco and recreated their Eastern world with Orthodox churches. Now their elegant domes graced the neighborhood skyline and always gave Frank a pleasant feeling he called beauty. He'd discovered at some point that their theology was similar to Catholicism.

Frank viewed Father Al as a worthy man. The way he listened, the way he seemed to carry a simple wisdom. But mostly the way he was protecting Elena from Anya. For that reason, the old man was his ally.

Soon he was near home. He continued on Geary, past the middle school and high school, heading toward the house where he'd grown up and where he and Fred still lived. He parked on the steep block, curbed his wheels, and sat a minute before getting out, looking at the vestibule of their house—dark, even in daylight. The pink decorator lights cast a shadow on the angular stairwell.

He got out of the cab and waved at Mr. Lui, his neighbor, who was sweeping out front of his house and Frank's. Mr. Lui liked to sweep in the mid-morning. He gave Frank a big smile and then a bit of wisdom: "A nice day for a surprise," he said.

"Like my beard," Frank said, jesting. He rubbed his face and chin, where a day-old beard prickled his fingers. He left Mr. Lui nodding and smiling; once again, his neighbor hadn't gotten his joke.

Frank entered the foyer and smelled the scent of last night's dinner: spaghetti with fungi and a strong-smelling French cheese. He and Fred typically ate late, and more often than not leftovers from the bistro, eaten in the living room, sitting on opposite ends of their old tweed couch—where Mom and Dad used to sit sipping their tea or wine, where they once opened Christmas presents.

He opened the front door, went inside, and sat down in Fred's easy chair, still thinking about his brother and this house they shared. The house had watched the turning from a family of four to an older brother caring for a younger one. It had witnessed the joys of birthdays and holidays—especially Frank's beloved Christmas, with singing and, always, Ma's cream pastries. It was this house on the Avenues, with its backyard treehouse that Fred had built for him, that gave him constancy, that had pulled him through the hardship of losing their parents. He climbed that eucalyptus tree when he needed to get above things, sitting inside adoring the raging red-violet *passiflora*, passion vine, that grew wildly over the fence separating his house from Mr. Lui's. The cool, foggy summers of the outer Richmond suited him, sheltered him in a protective layer. He could count on the fog's cyclical comings and goings. Summer morning fog burned off mid-morning and rolled in again in the afternoon, leaving a cool blanket of moisture; it even continued into the fall, like now.

And he could count on Fred too, of course, who was more than a brother; he was a fatherly figure who'd tended to all Frank's needs while holding down a responsible job in the restaurant. How had he done it?

Frank was in awe of his older brother, who'd raised him, managed to go to culinary school, and still had time for him, like today at the Cinderella. He sometimes wondered if Fred was ashamed that Frank drove a cab; that he wasn't all that he could be; that he drank too much as a teenager. He hadn't gone to college. In fact, he had no marketable skill sets, which was part of why he'd taken up driving. He pictured the little pouch in the dark cave of his glove compartment and felt a bit like a man waiting to fill his heart with a purpose.

Even though Fred had listened to him today at the Cinderella, he had told him to drop the girl. It was clear he wanted Frank out of it. Frank couldn't tell him everything—not about being witness to a woman dissolving in front of his eyes. He hadn't told him about the one threatening to kill the other, either. He feared that Fred would think he was crazy and feel worried, or feel that he'd somehow failed him, and he didn't want that.

Frank wanted some answers about this spell he seemed to be under, and not the one Fred had given him. He thought about Jane again, and a plan of action imprinted in his mind. Might she be able to interpret what was going on for him? She had been a breath of fresh air—so easy to talk with, and so kind. He liked the way she talked about things—ideas and nature. He felt comfortable in her presence. And she'd said she was a spiritual teacher, too. Maybe that meant she'd be willing to help him.

"New cells implant in the caterpillar, more and more, until the old cells can't survive," she'd said. "The imaginal cells clump together in the chrysalis and eventually, voilà, a butterfly." When Frank thought about this process of transformation now, he realized maybe he wanted that for himself. He had her card. He would call her and ask if he could come by for a visit.

First, however, he picked up the landline and called the dispatcher to say he was taking the rest of the day off.

He found Jane's number and dialed. Waited. What would he say? That he wanted to talk about imaginal cells or snowy plovers? No, he'd tell her he'd seen some phenomena that he couldn't understand, couldn't explain, and could she be a sounding board for him?

"Hello," a soft yet direct voice answered.

Nervous, Frank launched into an explanation of who he was and why he was calling.

"Yes, of course I remember you," she said kindly when he finally stopped talking. "The ride from the airport to Mill Valley . . . you were so generous to stop for me to see the snowy plovers."

"Endangered, aren't they?" Frank said. "Sand dunes up to our knees."

He heard her chuckle lightly, then pause. She waited for him to go on.

"*I* feel endangered now," he said, "and I've been thinking about the butterflies and their amazing transformation. The imprints you talked about. Mine are knocking on my door . . . or maybe knocking me out." He didn't know what in the hell he was talking about.

"And?" she said.

"I need to understand why I'm so deep in this thing. Can I come see you?"

"Please," she said. "The house below the watershed. The sign will read 'Retreat Center.'"

"Yes, I remember the heart-shaped driveway."

"Any time after lunch," she said. "I'll be here."

CHAPTER 12: *Ode to a Salamander*

Outfitted in black bicycle pants, fluorescent yellow vest, bike shoes, and helmet, Frank began the twenty-mile ride to Jane's. With the fog dissipating, the partial sun brightened his ride through Seacliff and then along the coastline in the Presidio toward the Golden Gate.

Gliding over the west side of the bridge, he viewed the open Pacific Ocean and put the city behind him. He let out a sigh of relief and watched a container ship make its way under the gate. He wondered what it might be like to be on that ship.

After he carried his bike down the stairs under the north tower and rode downhill to Bridgeway, his thoughts turned to Jane and what she thought about his coming. She'd sounded happy to hear from him on the phone.

Soon enough he was through Sausalito and onto the bike path that led to Mill Valley. *Piece of cake*, he thought, letting the moist air refresh him. When he reached downtown Mill Valley, he stopped to get a coffee at Peet's before heading west out of town to Blithedale Canyon, where large redwoods guarded each side of the road. He curved through the narrow, dark lanes of giant trees, immersed in the depths of the enchanted forest with its chorus of bird song.

He had ridden almost to the end of the Blithedale Canyon by the time he saw the sign announcing the ranch and retreat center up ahead. The shade turned day into shadow, reminding him of Elena and witnessing her killing the duck with such grace. It had been almost like a kiss.

At the end of the road, he entered the retreat center where he had taken Jane weeks earlier, not expecting then that he would return to ask her for help, not expecting she might be the only person who would understand. That all seemed a time very long ago—before Anya, or Elena, or Father Al.

The sign at the entrance to the circular drive warned against non-retreatants entering and reminded visitors to respect the silence. Once again, the heart-shaped lawn in front of the huge house floored him. Jane had told him her uncle had created it for his bride, his love. For Frank it was a Taj Mahal—majestically awesome. He wondered if he would ever feel strongly enough about someone to erect a memorial to that love.

He parked his bike on the far side of the house on a gravel patch leading up to a side stairway and a wraparound porch—the kind you'd be more likely to see in the South than in Northern California. Then he approached the front door, where he'd deposited her luggage the last time.

The door was ajar and he could see inside the foyer. He shifted his weight from foot to foot before pressing the doorbell, which sounded like a temple bell. Peering inside, he saw a grand wooden stairway in the center of the space—a stairway for the stars. To the right, on a marble-topped buffet, was a seated golden Buddha. His lips turned upward with the gentlest smile.

It was quiet inside. No one in sight.

He pushed the white buzzer again and waited with the vibrations of the temple bell. This time a dog came, sniffed his hand, and waited there beside him. Frank felt happy for the companionship of the white mutt. He fluffed its ears and the softness reminded him of the moleskin pouch sitting in his glove compartment.

Soon enough he saw Jane hurrying down the stairs, barefoot, casually dressed in sweats. She was stunning, even more so for being dressed casually. Curly blond hair framed her face, giving her a youthful look. She was not that much older than he was—maybe in her early mid-thirties, Fred's age. Thinking of her as an older sister made him feel more comfortable.

"Hello," she said. "That's Mutter. He likes you."

She motioned Frank toward a small cushioned couch on the great porch. The dog followed and sat at his feet.

"First let me get you a glass of water," she said, heading for the door. "I'll be just a minute."

"Thank you." He smiled at her, feeling shy. His hands sat nervously on his spandex capris. Her beauty and graceful energy moved him. He hadn't met anyone like her before.

Upon returning, she handed him the water and then sat down next to him on the porch couch.

He took a long gulp of water, then said, "I thought you might be off on an adventure."

"Always." She smiled. "So, what's going on?"

"I've been experiencing some strange things lately, seeing things that maybe aren't even there," he said slowly. "It's kind of like I've met some witches and a Cinderella."

"Like you're in a fairy tale."

He nodded. "Yes, it seems I'm part of some mysterious story I don't know how to explain." He told her about the two bizarre women and the girl—how she was being taught by one of the women and how she was under threat from the other; how he worried for her; how he'd become enmeshed in this world somehow. He even told her about Cornelius the magician.

"You take people to heart," she said. "Look how sensitive you were to my needs when you picked me up at SFO." She reached out her hand to him.

He took her hand and mulled this over. All he'd done was allow her to check out the snowy plovers. But she pushed forward, telling him he was different from others, repeating that he took people to heart. No one had ever told him that before and he liked it. Was that why he was drawn to her? Why he was here? Maybe she could see him the way others couldn't.

"Thank you," he finally said.

"You want to help the girl. Maybe you're caught in her spell, the way we are sometimes with others."

"I do. I am. But what if I fail her?"

"The worst thing for you is to doubt yourself," she admonished. "You're already helping her, aren't you?"

This got his attention, and he wasn't sure he could answer. Was he helping Elena?

She interrupted his thoughts by suggesting they go on a walk. "I want to show you the grounds. The trees are where I think best." She stood up. "Let me get my shoes. We'll talk more on the path as we walk." She looked at his cleated bike shoes. "Can you walk uphill in those?"

"I think so," he said, though he'd never tried hiking in bike shoes before.

She reached inside the foyer, and when she straightened back up she was holding a pair of women's Nikes and another pair of men's shoes for him. "My uncle's," she said.

He put them on and they almost fit—maybe only one size too big. "Not bad," he said.

He followed her down a path to the pond where redwoods mingled with pines, reaching and creating a canopy overhead. Birds sang and jumped from branch to branch.

"My temple," she said. "I do my best work here."

"What is your work, again?"

"I am a spiritual teacher and ecologist. We lead silent retreats in nature—four to ten days," she said, "with guest teachers."

Frank wasn't sure about being silent for ten days. That scared him. What if sadness overtook him? He would sit there and think of his parents and that would be hard. What if he couldn't stifle his sobs or choke them down like he'd tried to do with Fred that morning at the bakery? Likely he'd just cry out in the crowd and feel embarrassed. He'd disturb the silence of others. Worse was the possibility that his nightmares would come back—images of the crash, his parents' death. He needed to be able to distract himself. No, he didn't think silence was for him. Not now, anyway.

Inhaling the fragrance of trees—tall pines with scents of pepper and cinnamon, laurels, and redwood trees growing in circular clusters—brought him away from his thoughts. He craned to see small creatures flicking through the branches. A crow alighted on one large branch and then jumped off just as easily. Frank imagined the exertion made in that little jump and thought for the first time that he could feel the crow's tiny heart pumping so vigorously to make the jump.

The path led to a pond. When they reached the water's edge, he stopped and looked down to see small animals, prehistoric-seeming, swimming and diving under and over each other, playing, drawing their arcs in the water.

"And here you see the Life Force at your reach," Jane said, "the cycles of life and transformation right in this little pond."

"Transformations—that's what I wonder about, like tadpoles turning into frogs."

"And frogs into princes," she said.

That got his attention; he laughed. Frank turned her words over in his mind as he watched the tadpoles swimming and dive-bombing.

"Tell me more about these witches and your Cinderella—or is it *The Princess and the Frog*?" She smiled.

He described Elena and Anya, then he told her about the women fighting like cats, the cursing and spitting; how one of them vowed to kill the other to protect the girl; and how one had burst into smoke before his very eyes. Then he admitted how crazy he thought it all sounded.

"I would trust your perception," she said, touching his shoulder. He sighed.

"Tell me more about the turning to smoke," she prompted.

"It was the two of them arguing, and then—bam, smoke, like a magic trick. It was so real, but then I thought it couldn't be. I think that's why I'm here, why I wanted to talk to you. I feel like I'm living in a dream. Like I'm at the edge of sleep but I'm wide-awake."

"Yes, you see, there are many alternative ways of seeing this," Jane said casually. "Maybe one of those women did dissolve before your eyes. Maybe she is a ghost and you're called to be a witness."

He bent over to get a look at his reflection in the pool; Jane leaned over too so that they stood side by side, their images mingling with the salamanders, tadpoles, and creatures that seemed to be rowing or gliding. He watched their movements in and around the mirror image of their faces, as if they too were disappearing and reappearing in a timeless space.

"This is beautiful," he said. "What are those insects?"

"Water spiders."

He smiled. "They look like they're skating."

Jane returned to the issue at hand. "Have you had experiences like this before—things disappearing before your eyes?"

"Sometimes I can see my mom, who died when I was eight, and hear her speaking to me," Frank said. "It seems kind of normal to me now. But no, I've never seen things disappear. It's more the opposite." He remembered all the things he'd found in his life—keys, a passenger's cell, a lost luggage at SFO, a teacher's attendance sheet, an overshot ball, twenty-four school sweatshirts. "I often find lost things. But just regular things."

"So you're gifted in this way. You see things that many don't—like the smoke."

He straightened up, letting her words sink in. It brought him to the day his parents died. He'd been up early that day to wish them well on their road trip to Big Sur to eat at Nepenthes, the place where his father had proposed to his mother.

"Tell me what else," she said, as if sensing there was more.

"I knew the day my mom and dad left in the car I'd never see them again"—he paused, his head down—"that there'd be an accident." A knot gripped his throat. He had never told anyone this, not even Fred. His eyes began to sting, forecasting tears. He paused, swallowed, opened his eyes as wide as he could, and took a breath,

"And I didn't try to stop them from leaving. I used to stay awake at night to fight off the terror of seeing the way they got slammed into by the guy who ran a red light. I ran it over and over and over, asking myself why I hadn't stopped them from going. I could have feigned ill health; I could have staged a tantrum or told them what I saw. But I didn't do anything. I blame myself. I feel like I killed them. The only thing left to me is to be a good driver."

They stood in silence. Jane took his wrist and held it like a bracelet, gently and loosely. "I'm so sorry for your loss," she said.

Those tears he'd tried so hard to hold back the moment before slipped from the corners of his eyes silently.

"All this grief you hold." She looked straight into his wet eyes. "You didn't kill them, you know."

Hearing these words immediately brought loud sobs. Tears gushed from Frank's eyes, and his chest heaved as if his heart would break open.

Jane watched, waited. When he found his natural rhythm, she handed him a tissue and smiled. "You're a good driver—I can attest to that."

He smiled, regaining himself.

She had validated that he hadn't dreamed the woman dissolving into smoke; that he hadn't been responsible for his parents' death; that he was holding grief. Her words allowed him to take a deep breath and create a sense of calm, the first he'd experienced in a while.

"Do you think it's just a coincidence that Anya and Cornelius the magician and you ended up in my cab in the first place?" he asked her.

"I don't," she said. "You are attuned in this way. That's all."

He stared at her.

"Simply put, it was the right time for us to show up in your life. Or let me put it another way: You were called to bear witness to the girl killing the duck, the dissolving, Cornelius, all of it."

Frank frowned, unsure.

"In Greek, it's *kairos*. The stars aligned."

"The stars aligned," he repeated, feeling those words inside his mouth.

"And something was revealed to you," Jane said.

"And what about Elena? What does this ugly woman showing up claiming to be her mother reveal to her?"

"This is Elena's fate. Something is shifting for her."

Frank's eyebrows rose in question.

"Something like that happened to me and set me in a new direction once," Jane said.

"What do you mean?"

"One day I woke up and saw how everything would happen for me in my life," she said. "It was a transition for me."

"Will you tell me the story?" Frank asked eagerly.

"I was twenty-four," she said, "and sitting in a meadow in Yosemite, when a beautiful buck approached. His antlers reached toward the trees and granite cliffs, though curved with many turns and bifurcations. We stared at each other. Time stood still, or there was no time. The buck whispered, *This moment is made of every moment: the present, the past, and the future and beyond.*"

Frank exhaled in wonder.

"A transformative moment for me," she said simply. "My life's work: to be in the moment. Likely the woman appearing marks a transition for Elena too."

Her words, though mysterious, made some sense to Frank. He was called to be a witness to some great transformation. Though still nervous, he felt assured that he was on the right path. Being there with her—and the trees and the garden and the water creatures—helped him feel more alive, less lonely. For him, Jane was a kind soothsayer. She said the words he could never find— words that felt truthful, poetic, and magical. His heart lifted.

Jane was laughing now, her blond curls bouncing with her. "Frank, what if you let go of how you define yourself? What would that be like?"

Frank thought of the ways he'd defined himself—the man who drove a cab; the adolescent who drank too much; the kid who lost his mother. And now, the man who was a witness. Was she asking him to open up to other ways of seeing himself—to allow himself to be more complex? Was he a guy who saw the boundless? A guy who cried? He shook his head. Maybe—he wasn't convinced.

"If you could be someone or something else," Jane said, "what would you be?"

"I'd be a jellyfish," he said, "maybe a frog prince." He looked into the pond at the swimming creatures.

"Exactly; you'd be something formless," she confirmed. "You are opening to a more spiritual dimension."

"You mean like being in *the flow*."

"Like having a premonition about what's about to happen. It's mercurial, like in a fairy tale."

"Exactly," he said, thinking how Anya had attached herself to him and how he had known in his bones that she was lying.

"A fairy tale has wrapped itself around you." She seemed to understand exactly what he was going through, was able to put words to this strange experience.

"Exactly," Frank said again. He liked the word *mercurial*. He had always loved that word—always associated it with the wind, with magic. *Mercurial* gave Frank a thrill and opened a longing within him for this magic.

Jane nodded at him. He realized they were speaking the same language—the language of spirituality, with its potential to allow for change and transformation, for seeing things in new ways. That was the magic he'd yearned for as an adolescent, and now Jane was affirming that possibility.

"Imagine that we all are working toward creating a more evolved version of ourselves, like the butterfly in the chrysalis," Jane said. "In producing cells that could destroy it, the butterfly actually creates itself. Through destruction of our former selves, we create a new self. But only if we're open to the change."

It felt to Frank that something was shattering, perhaps a chrysalis of old beliefs. He looked down at the tadpoles. The only time he'd heard reference to destruction and creation as two sides of a coin was in a high school science class, when Mr. Quelley told them that volcanoes destroyed and created at the same time.

"But what would Anya or that other woman be creating in her dissolving?" he asked.

Jane shrugged. "In the end there are no explanations. There's only a story."

"Yup, this is quite a story." Frank let his eyes sweep the width of the pool, staring at the tadpoles with their bulging eyes and the rowing creatures with their oars, all of them holding their own magic.

"This story is still unfolding, so there is a lot you don't know when you're in the middle of something—right?" Jane said.

Frank nodded, still gazing into the water.

When he finally looked up, Jane was no longer beside him. He scanned the perimeter of the teeming pool. Above the pond, on a large stone bridge, she sat on a wooden bench. She smiled and waved, motioning for him to join her. She pointed to a simple way around the rectangular pond. He followed the path and crossed the bridge, marveling at the Garden of Eden surrounding him.

She offered him a seat beside her on the sculpted bench.

"I've never seen anything like this. Paradise, isn't it?"

"These gardens, Angor Gardens, were the dream of the founder of this place," she said.

"Anger?" he repeated, confused.

"No, *Ango,* like the Buddhist concept of a peaceful abode," she said. "Like your taxi, Frank."

He looked at her, surprised.

"Your taxi is the peaceful abode of the traveler," she said.

"What?"

"You don't believe me."

He shook his head. "I just don't understand."

"Your taxi is a sanctuary for the weary traveler, a sacred place where people, visitors, and natives alike feel safe enough to dream."

He faced her. "Oh . . . you think?"

Her eyes were clear and reflected light. "Did the actor feel safe enough to sing and play this morning?"

"I've never thought of it like that before," Frank said. Then he pictured Henry O, delighting in his constancy; Anya, looking for the girl and spilling her ugliness; Jane, the spiritual guide, turning him inside-out like a shaman. He contemplated the women who'd recently entered his life—at least four: the two witches, Elena, and now Jane. He hadn't had any women in his life since his mom.

"So many women in this story," Jane said, mirroring his thoughts. "The feminine has unveiled herself."

"I'll say," he said. "I don't have a clue about the feminine. I was raised by my brother."

"Don't dismiss yourself so easily," she said. "The feminine is related to a deep knowing. We all have it."

Again, he liked how direct she was, and how she was sticking up for him.

They got up and continued across another stone bridge on a trail toward the Mount Tam watershed. The path was steep and muddy in parts. He followed her and the white dog, Mutter, who knew the trail by heart.

When they reached the top, they walked in the shadow of Mount Tam.

The road was wide, a fire road. He imagined a time when the Coast Miwok lived here. Quiet kissed him. The earth softened him. Underfoot was a blanket of golden duff. The hillside glowed orange in the sunlight. They saw no one.

Eventually, they made a loop through redwoods, down through paved streets with houses, and back to Jane's stunning heart-shaped lawn.

"I never get tired of this love garden," she said.

He looked at her. In her presence he felt like a kid again, free to explore snowy plovers, salamanders, rowing insects, sleeping princesses, and peaceful abodes. In the company of the deep reflecting pools and sheltering trees, he felt happy.

When they got to the porch, she invited him to stay as long as he wanted but said she had to leave to get to a meeting in town. She'd been invited to lead a seminar in nature as a spiritual practice at Dominican College.

"Thank you," he said. "I may commune with the salamanders a little bit more before I go." A name for a poem ran through his mind: "Ode to a Salamander." *Salamander in an overgrown pool,* he thought. *Small boy, I will call you Buddha.*

As these words came to him, he knew more of the poem dwelled in his heart and would come forth soon. He thought to tell Jane but decided against it.

"Isn't nature wonderful?" She laughed, her smile open and inviting.

"Maybe we can walk again sometime," he said.

"Yes, I would like that," she said.

CHAPTER 13: *Acorns*

*T*his morning, en route to the house on Taraval Street, Elena cuts through the park at 36th Avenue, hoping De-doo will be home today. She never saw him yesterday, and she missed him.

Passing Spreckels Lake, she stops and examines the wind sails on the miniature sailboats along the edge of the small pond. The little boats are not wind-powered, although it looks that way to her at first. These are toys, activated by batteries attached to their owners' belts. The owners aren't children at all but boy-men, playing at the lake. She shakes, not at all sure why she trembles at the unusual sight. Perhaps because of her dream last night, of the bad man rushing for her.

In the dream, Elena saw herself as an infant swaddled in a white blanket. There was a ruckus nearby, people screaming. A man in an oversize coat was running fast toward her, scaring her, holding a knife in his hand. She thought he wanted to gut her, skin her alive, and eat her heart. When his coat opened, she saw it was not a man at all, but Anya. She froze in her dream, and in that frozen moment Baba Vera appeared. She twirled and spun so fast she generated a spark that ignited a flame that burned Anya's image away and then she said, "Dearie, dearie, do it cheery."

Elena woke up wanting to study this strange dream, to hold on to it, to put it in her pocket, but it immediately slipped away like mist. Now, however, as she walks in the park, she remembers— remembers how Baba protected her in the dream just as she has done in real life. Elena's heart warms with feelings of love for Baba and De-doo, who have taught her such diverse skills and given her new challenges and tools. They have been her guides.

But what could this strange dream mean? She pats her doll and thanks Kukla for her company as she scurries past the men with their boats.

When Elena gets to the log-framed house on Taraval, she enters through the workshop, but Dedushka Victor is not there. She feels disappointed; she was hoping to see his kind face. She feels affection for him. Yet her heart flitters, too, like a butterfly passing. A sweet sadness prevails, like the last scents of jasmine on a fading trellis.

She enters the middle room and hangs her cape and red sack. The scent of dry flowers and pepper float in the air.

Finally, she opens the door into the inner sanctum and sets to work straightening the table where grinding tools and a mortar and pestle sit. Baba has been grinding herbs.

"The acorns are plump now, child," Baba says upon seeing her. "You must harvest them tonight." Baba sits on the second bunk with all three guinea pigs in her lap.

"Yes, Baba, I've been noticing some here and there on my way here. But how can I harvest them in one night? Is there a particular place where I should go? Is there a reason why they must be harvested tonight?"

"The moon smiles tonight—ha, ha, ha," Baba says. "Though your spirit may not know where, your feet will carry you."

Baba smiles, her mouth wide and glowing, and Elena sees in her the graceful beauty of a very old grandmother—not the usual sort she's seen at Our Lady on Sundays, old women who seem to frown with worry. Baba is different, an ancient grandma of the earth, stars, and sea.

This is not the first time she's seen Baba this way. Elena recalls her wearing this beatific look on the day Kukla fell out of her pocket. Baba's smile eases her heart.

"Collect them for a bread," Baba says, not answering Elena's other questions. "I have a hankering for acorn bread."

"Acorn bread?" Elena asks, never having eaten it, never mind seen it, before. An unusual request, and a departure from the carving of meats, killing of animals, or tending to the garden.

"Yes, I want bread made from pounds of ripe, plump acorns. And you will begin tonight. You'll start by gathering them by the hundreds. Then you will bring them here and grind them using the mortar and pestle." She points to the grinding tools in excitement. Her bony legs and long toes wriggle. The guinea pigs jump from her lap, one by one, as if she's given them a silent command.

Elena can't imagine grinding pounds of acorns in the small mortar sitting on the table. How many hundreds would that be? A thousand? Grinding one or two acorns at a time would take forever in a small grinder. This task seems absurd, and yet Baba's given her challenging tasks like this before and Elena's not only managed but done well.

"You have been a good daughter," Baba says, rising to stand next to her.

"Thank you," Elena says, hyperaware of the compliment and not sure how to respond. She knows for sure that she will not challenge Baba on the idea of the acorn bread. She knows it's another test that will make her stronger.

Baba tells her again that the acorns must be harvested at night. "From the grove," she says, but elaborates no further.

Elena thinks of Oak Glen, at the easternmost end of Golden Gate Park, near the panhandle.

"Be sure only to gather the very plumpest ones, which will grind more easily into flour," Baba says, drooling.

Elena feels disgusted by her expression and recalls her insatiable hunger for pork tenders and meats.

"And beware of the wild creatures that sweep into the night," Baba warns.

"What wild creatures, Baba?" Elena trembles, remembering her dream.

"Beware," is all she says, looking into Elena's eyes.

Baba's eyes, liquid gray diamonds, stare straight into Elena for a long moment; then she diverts her gaze to the small cedar chest De-doo made for her, which rests on a table near the butcher block. Elena has never dared to peek inside the chest.

She shivers at the memory of her dream as Baba swoops over to the cedar chest, opens it, and collects three small jars from it. Whiffs of wild laurel float into the room as she puts small handfuls of dried spices into a tightly woven purse—spices she has collected, drained of their nectar, chopped, and ground with a pestle.

Baba hands her the woven purse filled with herbs. "You will need these tonight when you gather the acorns by the light of the rising full moon."

"Thank you, Baba," Elena says, a bit confused. "But why do I need special herbs for tonight?"

Baba doesn't respond, but the scent of the herbs refreshes Elena and gives her reassurance that Baba has a way of knowing—and has her back.

Elena watches as she dips three bony fingers into an amber glass that looks like a votive candle and scoops out the paste.

"I have harvested these with my own hands," she says with a gleeful look in her eyes. She approaches Elena, hand outstretched, rubs the creamy salve onto Elena's forehead, murmuring some indecipherable sounds and holding Elena's face in both hands. Her gleeful eyes, like a still pond reflecting a moonbeam, penetrate into Elena's being, while enchanting scents of wild sage and bay laurel, rose petals, peppermint, cinnamon, and a dash of cayenne breathe out into the room.

Though she feels a prickly sensation on her skin, in her heart Elena experiences bliss. The salve gives off the scent of the forest and cleans away worrisome thoughts the way a wind can pull dried leaves from a live oak. Fears about things like gathering hundreds of acorns in one night or the roaming of strange creatures in the night melt away.

I am well prepared, she thinks to herself. *No task is impossible with Kukla by my side.* Feeling light and at ease, she remembers Father Al singing nursery rhymes as well as his Kyries to her as a child. The words of "Kalinka," a Russian folk song he hasn't sung to her for years, rises up in her memory.

> *Little red berry,*
> *Little red berry of mine!*
> *In the garden is a little raspberry,*
> *My little raspberry!*
>
> *Under the green pine tree*
> *Lay me down to sleep*
> *Oh, lyuli, lyuli, oh, lyuli, lyuli,*
> *Lay me down to sleep.*

Humming "*oh, lyuli, lyuli, oh lyuli, lyuli,*" Elena goes on with her chores of sweeping and cleaning, putting the late-autumn garden to rest—picking off the dead leaves from the living plants, pulling up the dead roots and bulbs, pulling dried herbs she knows will be reborn in spring, and placing bulbs in dark paper sacks to sleep until next planting. Elena loves this tending.

As she finishes up, she picks some fresh sleeves of cabbage for Piglet. Hiding them behind her back, she heads to his little house at the end of the yard. "Piglet, *oh lyuli, oh lyuli!*" she calls. "Come out; I have a surprise for you!"

But Piglet doesn't come.

Elena peeks inside and sees that she's not there. She's nowhere to be found—not in her little house, not out in the yard. Only the guinea pigs and the last of the harvest—the carrots, kale, beets, and potatoes—are there.

When she comes inside, Elena sets down her pail and warms herself for a moment at the black furnace where thick black coffee sits steaming in a blue enamel coffeepot. She then brings the harvest to the sink and is preparing to wash it when she hears the door open.

She turns and is surprised to see Dedushka Victor enter the inner sanctum.

"Elena," he says, beaming. "You have been gathering food, tending the garden. Singing a sweet lullaby."

"De-doo, you're home!" She runs to him as he places a tall, lush plant on the butcher table.

He hugs her, then gestures to the plant. "A plant for Baba," he says, "from Mendocino."

Elena looks around, half-expecting to see Baba in the hutch, waiting for lunch, but she's nowhere to be seen. It's unusual for Elena and De-doo to be alone in the kitchen.

"Where is Baba?" she asks.

"She's out on business," he says quickly.

Elena didn't realize she'd left. She wonders if she took Piglet and Koza with her.

"Are Piglet and Koza with her?" She has an unsettling thought that Anya has taken the beloved animals, and Baba too. Sadness threatens to overwhelm her.

De-doo pauses, his hand lifting to massage his bearded chin. He looks like Santa Claus.

"Please tell me about Anya, De-doo. Does she have Piglet and Koza? Will she hurt them? Who is she, anyway?"

"Anya . . . is a distant relation from Russia," he says, stopping short of saying something else.

"Oh, De-doo, how can you who are so nice . . ." She stops herself from asking how he could have such a horrible relative, worried that he will confirm that he and Baba are related to Anya and that her worst fear—that she is Elena's mother—is true. And what if she has something to do with the animals' absence from the yard, and Baba's too?

"How nice to have a visitor from Russia," she says instead.

"She's the devil from Hell!" De-doo says. "Evil." He turns toward the pot of dark Russian coffee on the stove. "But you don't need to worry about her. We will take care of her."

"I worry for our safety," Elena says tremulously. "I will be happy to have her gone. Will she be returning to Russia?"

"Baba knows how to handle her," is all De-doo says.

"What will she do?"

"She will dissolve her, if she must."

"Dissolve?" Elena gapes. "But how, De-doo?"

"These are the mysteries of witches," he says. "You will see."

Hearing this response, Elena just stands there, mouth hanging open in surprise. She considers how Baba can foresee her thoughts; how she plays with herbs, harvests stems and roots, cuts and chops and makes pastes and salves; how she lives in a hut-style house and has a magical broom. Suddenly Elena feels not only awe for Baba and her magical gifts but also validated. *Of course she's a witch*, she thinks. She touches her forehead; the salve Baba placed there awakens and sends its peaceful feeling through her again. Thus calmed, she lifts the blue enamel pot, fills De-doo's waiting cup with thick, muddy coffee, and hands it to him.

"And Piglet? Koza?"

"They have gone to live up north," he says.

A storm cloud forms inside of her, readying itself to burst forth with energy, allowing her to speak more freely. "Are they safe, De-doo?"

"Yes, they are safe," he says. He takes a sip of his coffee.

"Things are coming to a head, aren't they, De-doo?" she says. "It seems time for me to know more." She tells him how Baba visited her in a dream last night and saved her from a grave danger.

"Yes, Elena, Baba has powers beyond what you can dream of, and now she is about to finish the story of this wayward creature," he explains. "When she does, Anya's curse upon your mother will be finished."

Elena feels confused; her only reference for her mother is the letter she keeps tucked safely away in her book. She silently repeats the words of the letter to herself to see if she has missed something about a curse, but nothing reveals itself.

"I have to ask you something. Was Anya the reason my mother left me with Father Al and returned to Russia?" Elena feels a relief at having asked this question. She looks at Victor.

"Yes, your dear mother Masha brought you away from the wicked one before her leaving."

"Leaving?"

"Yes, your mother was ill and knew she would die soon. I'm sorry for her illness, and for your loss."

"Thank you, De-doo." Though Elena has always known this, no one has told her so directly before. Clarity comingles with familiar sorrow.

"You are a good girl, Elena," he says. "Babushka has taught you well. I am not worried about you. You will be safe. You have our blessing." He presses his finger on her forehead where Baba placed the salve. The way he blesses her makes her think they're preparing her for more changes. Maybe they're saying goodbye. She feels sad at this thought, and wonders if she'll ever see Piglet again. She wonders about her life without them.

He leaves the inner sanctum of their house. She watches him walk slowly through the middle room to his shop, coffee in hand, shutting the door behind him. She wonders what has prompted him to speak so freely. Could it be he thinks of her as more ready, more worldly-wise?

The skull and bones of Baba's ancestors on the wall reflect the afternoon sun, as if they are animated. She swipes her hand over her eyes, wondering if she really sees them breathing.

She stokes the fire, adds more kindling, and watches it take, letting the flames shoot up. Before she closes the furnace door, she adds a large piece of oak. She watches and when the heat rises, she gets the iron fryer and sautés the veggies, adding handfuls of herbs as she does.

When the vegetables are ready, she sets out the bowls and spoons on the wooden table for their dinner and then passes into the middle room, where she slips on her cape and slides her hands through the strap of her red shoulder bag.

She enters De-doo's workshop. He's sitting in his chair, head down, holding his black coffee—cold now. She pats his sleeping head. "Goodbye De-doo."

CHAPTER 14: *The Bistro*

Frank showed up on Sacramento Street after his long day, which started with the bike ride to Mill Valley, a walk around the salamander pond, and then picking up Henry O. He'd managed a short nap at home before heading to the restaurant, where he now sat at a back table, studying the menu.

Frank felt lighter for Jane's words. The primordial-seeming creatures in the pond had impressed him greatly—so much so that he had indeed finished creating a poem about them in his head at Jane's and then rehearsed it on his bike ride back to the city. He wrote it on a napkin now:

"Ode to a Salamander"
Salamander in an overgrown pool.
Small boy, I will call you Buddha.
You don't know where you are going
or if you have a future
or whether you'll still work in old age.
You just torpedo your small, sleek body
through the overgrown water—
that is, when you don't just stand still.

He wondered if he was, like the salamander, a sleek one who torpedoed into waters over his head, a small boy who didn't know where he was going or if he had a future.

He perused the menu, half-expecting to find grilled salamander there, but instead his eyes focused on duck with elderberry sauce, duck confit, duck liver pate.

"I'll tell your brother you're here, Frank," the familiar waiter said politely. "Are you expecting a guest?" he asked, pointing at the extra plates. Frank looked around the dining room—a compact room filled to capacity with happy diners, drinking and chatting.

"No, just me, thank you." Frank wondered if he'd ever have a guest to dine with him. Maybe Jane. They would continue talking about new cells, the feminine, and butterflies. She'd told him he had a special sensitivity; that his cab was a sacred space; that pollywogs were an example of the life cycle. He could feel her calmness, see her sitting on her porch. He could hear her being direct, telling him what she thought. Maybe this combination of calmness and directness was something to strive for. He'd call her again, maybe invite her to dinner, introduce her to Fred.

Then he thought of Elena. Would she ever dine with him here? He couldn't imagine sitting with her in this setting. What would she say when she saw duck on the menu? What would he say? The image of her breaking the little duck's neck so easily made him quiver. He wouldn't have been able to offer to help skin the duck either. Would he speak to her in riddles, tell her how Anya disappeared, how the sisters fought over her? What would she think of his strange confession? Hadn't he baffled her enough already in the way he stood there like a ghost in the night—or, worse, a stalker?

He knew what Fred would say. Get over it. Or the kid was hungry. Or the kid's a hunter. Or, most likely, didn't I tell you to forget her? Frank tried to clear his head and focus on the good parts of the day—the meaningful conversation with Jane, the overdue bike ride, and the poem he wrote.

When the waiter asked if he was ready to order, Frank thought of wine—considered red, but could only think of duck's blood. So he ordered a bottle of house white, which was soon placed on the table in front of him. The waiter poured him a glass and put the bottle on ice.

By the time Fred joined him, the bottle of wine was empty and the other guests had cleared out. The faint lighting of the restaurant reflected on the green walls, making Frank feel as if he were a sea creature or maybe one of those funny-looking creatures in the small pond, underwater rowing in circles, eyes bulging, skimming water. He squinted, thinking maybe it was the wine playing with his head. He hadn't drunk this much alcohol in a while.

"Kenwood produced a good white wine that year," Fred said, fingering the label of the empty bottle. He removed his apron, which showed the smudges of fat, red sauces, the blood of the sacrifice. "Dude, you just drank a bottle!" he said, sitting down. "That'll be it for tonight."

"So I blew it, don't get on my case," Frank said, thinking how he'd broken their agreement. He felt like a shit.

Fred talked about the bustle in the kitchen and the crescendo of excitement to get everything out hot and crisp at the same time. "Tonight the duck was the favorite. We sold at least a dozen . . . maybe fifteen."

The talk of duck made Frank's stomach turn. "Where do you get them from, anyway?" he asked. He had a restless leg; he tried to quiet it.

"From Petaluma," Fred said. "Bring us Pellegrino, Michael," he told the waiter who had just returned, bringing a second setting to the table.

"Would you be taking your dinner now?" Michael asked, looking at the clock. It was ten.

"Yes, everything in the kitchen is all set; the crew's got it under control now. Thank you, Michael."

Michael left the table for the water.

"You don't need a menu, do you Frank?" Fred asked.

Frank's stomach was still churning over the thoughts of all those dead ducks; he knew he should order something to eat after that bottle of wine, but he didn't feel hungry.

"Fifteen servings of duck at this one restaurant on this one evening," Frank said. "What if every restaurant in San Francisco served that many ducks this evening?" Silently, he was doing the math. If only ten restaurants in the city served ten each? That would be a hundred ducks. But there are several hundred restaurants—including Chinese restaurants, whose specialty is Peking ducks.

Fred frowned. "What the fuck is wrong with you? Take a chill pill. Thank God I didn't order a second bottle of wine. Get yourself some food!" he said as Michael poured the sparkling water.

Frank looked down, not wanting to meet Michael's eyes after that scolding.

"I'll come back," Michael said before slipping away.

Frank was more angry than hungry. Maybe at himself, for drinking too much. Maybe at Fred for calling him on it. "It's about duck," he cried, "goddamned duck!" He was not going to address Fred's dig about the drinking. He already felt badly enough about himself without his brother piling more on.

"Have you ever broken a duck's neck, Fred?" He looked up to see Fred's frown of concern. His eyes, caring and soft, looked the way they used to look when Frank was scared at night. Fred didn't answer but handed Frank the menu, which Michael must have put on the table without him noticing, and pointed to the veggie dishes.

When Michael returned, Fred ordered the seared duck special and Frank the pasta primavera with a side of croquettes. Michael left without another word.

Fred leaned forward. "What's going on here, Frank?"

Frank took another long sip of the cool sparkling water. "It's about the girl. I saw her kill a duck in the park."

"Yeah, you already told me about her at the bakery a few days ago."

"Yeah, after she fed the smallest duck, she snapped its neck." Frank thought he might start crying and he forced himself to regain his composure.

"Some girl!" Fred said. "Didn't I say you should stay away from her?"

"You don't get it, Fred. I want to protect her, like you protected me." He tried to explain, but even as he said it he knew it sounded ridiculous. He didn't even know her. She wasn't his sibling or his charge, like Frank was to Fred.

Fred looked down and buttered a piece of baguette. "Okay" was all he said, which had the opposite of a calming effect on Frank. He worried now that his brother most surely thought he was crazy and was just resigned to let him fall into the abyss.

"This girl," Frank tried to explain. "Elena's her name. She was raised by a priest and without a mother."

"Abandoned?" Fred asked, looking up at Frank for the first time. The sadness in his eyes betrayed his neutrality. Frank thought it made sense that he wasn't the only overly emotional one. They'd been scarred from losing their parents. Children without mothers stirred something for both of them.

"Look, Fred, I know it's hard to understand, but I'm drawn to help her, that's all. It probably looks like an obsession. Maybe it is."

Fred looked at his brother tenderly and said, "I had the best mom to raise me. You didn't get that chance. But you gave me a reason to go on." He cleared his throat. He reached out and put his hand on Frank's as a tear rose and spilled over.

Just then their food arrived, and Frank was grateful. He thought they might both be reduced to puddles on the floor right there in Fred's own restaurant if they were allowed to continue on.

Did he just say I gave him a reason to live? Frank chewed on this, absorbing its feel, new and slippery. Like the salamanders, it touched him deeply. He twirled his fork around the creamy fettucine in front of him and took a bite.

"Tell me more about your Hunter Girl," Fred said.

Frank blinked in surprise. It was the first time his brother had shown any kind of curiosity about Elena, the first time he'd not told Frank to let it go.

So he told Fred again about the strange woman just arrived from Russia: how she had him take her to the Russian church and asked him to wait for her; how he overheard her conversation with the old priest, demanding he give her the girl, and then about their chat in the cab about it afterwards; about his willingness to suspend judgment and then the inner feeling that she was lying.

For the first time, Fred heard him, seemed to take in the story rather than just wishing it away.

"Did the priest believe her?" he asked.

"No—he refused to give her any information, not even the girl's name, and he was sure she wasn't the woman who'd left the child at the church to begin with."

"Good call on his part," Fred said. "So what's next?" He cut a big hunk of duck with cardamom rub with his steak knife as he waited for Frank's response.

"Pellegrino—*in acqua, veritas*," Frank said. He picked up his water glass and clinked it with Fred's.

Frank looked at the defeathered bird on his brother's plate next to a heap of roasted carrots and potatoes. He looked at his own seemingly small plate of pasta, which appeared meek by comparison.

When Fred offered him a bite, he accepted the sweet, tender flesh under a crisp veneer as Fred's offering of love.

CHAPTER 15: *Pack Taurus*

As soon as he left the restaurant, Frank wanted another drink. Though he'd felt blessed by Fred just a moment before, his need for alcohol got the better of him. After rehab at twenty-one, he'd agreed only to drink with fine foods at the restaurant; tonight he'd slipped, blown it by drinking a bottle alone, and now he craved a beer to accompany him as he mulled over Fred's comment about how Frank had given meaning to his life all those years ago.

He left his taxi on the side street near the bistro where he'd parked before dinner and walked to a nearby Irish bar, his old hangout on Geary Boulevard where more than a few years ago he'd celebrated turning twenty-one and subsequently returned every night to drink. This was the joint where he'd come of age—and where he'd unraveled, too. His behavior there was the thing that had stopped his drinking. Ever since getting his taxi license, he'd kept his promise to Fred that he'd only drink at dinner—until tonight.

What the hell! I need a beer.

He thought of Elena's grace and decisiveness. Maybe she didn't need as much protecting as he'd imagined. Maybe he actually needed protecting more than she did.

The bar was dark when he entered. A TV showed college football.

The bartender nodded at Frank when he saw him.

"Long time no see," Hank said as Frank moved to his favorite seat at the bar, near the register and where the bartender hung out when not mixing drinks.

"Maybe four years," Frank said.

"Seems right." Hank was an old-timer, had probably been working there longer than Frank had been alive. He approached him on the other side of the bar. "Same?"

Frank nodded and the bartender poured a dark Guinness from the tap. Frank had grown up on the Irish dry stout. Loved it. Before he took a belt of it, he saw a heavyset guy at the other end of the bar stand up and walk toward him. *Christ, don't tell me that guy's still hanging around here!*

"Hey stranger," Pack said. "We're no good for you or something?"

They'd graduated in the same class, and during that year when Frank's drinking had been so out of control, Pack had matched him drink for drink.

"Pack Taurus," Frank said, recalling how much he disliked this guy.

"You bet your ass it's me—all six feet three of me," he preened, making himself even bigger.

Frank didn't say anything. That seemed to get Pack's ass.

"What's the matter, cat got your tongue?" the beefy man said, swiping Frank's shoulder with his fist so that Frank flinched.

Hank walked over. "Class reunion?"

"Yeah. But this guy ain't reuniting." Pack gestured with arms flying above his head in a spiraling wave.

"Sit down, Pack." Frank knew Pack was pissed at him for disappearing.

Pack plopped down on the stool next to him and nudged his chin in the direction of Frank's Guinness. "You still drink that shit?"

"Yeah, I love it."

"So what brings you to the hood?"

"Guinness. And to see Hank here." Frank looked toward the bartender as a kind of plea for help. Hank gave him a smile, stayed cool. Just stood there fixing his gaze on the two former schoolmates.

"You want your beer, Pack?" Hank looked down to the far end of the bar, where Pack's Bud wilted. No one else was at the bar.

Pack nodded, and Hank started to turn to fetch what must by now be warm beer, but Frank intercepted him with, "A cold one for Pack Taurus. It's on me."

"You got it." The cold beer in a frosted new mug arrived in front of Pack.

"You always were a generous bastard. Bastard, wasn't it? Raised by that queer brother, weren't you?" Pack swigged his beer, gulping down half the pint in one haul, his Adam's apple gyrating.

Frank envisioned punching him in the throat as the beer flowed down.

Pack wiped his dribbling mouth on the sleeve of his black sweatshirt. Beads of foam stuck to his sleeve like snot. "Fucking cold and delicious," Pack said, "just the way I like it." He tossed down the rest of the pint in one long gulp, then licked the foam from his generous lips.

"What you looking at, skinny boy?" Pack asked.

"Your pulsing, throbbing throat," Frank said.

"Huh! You insulting me?" Pack said, pushing his shoulder into Frank's head.

Frank thought about the pond and Jane, calming his urge to haul off and kill the guy. He thought about how Elena had so calmly and decidedly broken that duck's neck. He envied her.

Again he took a deep breath, for the sake of his brother, and for the moment the rage inside him quelled.

"So you still live with that fag?" Pack provoked.

"You never give up, do you?" Frank said, his heart pounding, pumping adrenaline. "You say that again, Pack Taurus, and—"

"And you'll what? You ponytailed fag, driving that yellow cab like it's a chariot. I seen you driving up and down Geary like you some charioteer. Huh, you nothing but the son of a whore." Pack poked a knuckle into Frank's throat.

Before he could get out any words, Frank stood up and punched him in the face. Of course, Pack was barely fazed. He hurled Frank to the floor and, with his size twelve boots, began kicking the hell out of him—first in the stomach, once, twice, three times.

The first kick seemed to root out Frank's insides. Each succeeding kick started a washing machine inside him, stirring the pain into a froth so he didn't know where it began or ended. All he could do was to try to protect his middle with his arms.

"The cops!" Hank shouted.

Pack stopped beating the shit out of Frank and looked up. There were no cops; Frank realized Hank was just trying to help. It worked.

"Take that, you son of a whore!" Pack spat, then walked back to his spot on the other side of the bar.

Hank helped Frank to his feet. "I'm sorry, kid. You know Pack has always had an inferiority complex. The Guinness is on me." Frank nodded and turned away, his mostly full Guinness still sitting and warming by the register.

Frank stumbled out of the place clutching his stomach. The pain, sharp as a knife, took his breath away. He knew he should get help but didn't want to call Fred—ashamed as he was of his drinking. If he could only remember where he'd parked the taxi. Had he driven from Sacramento Street to the bar? Or had he left it on the other side of the park? The bistro? The park? The bistro? The park?

He started toward the park, clutching his stomach. Every breath brought pain. He didn't want Fred to know he'd been at the pub. He looked around the street, not really sure where he was. He looked up to see the moon rising. He headed in that direction.

CHAPTER 16: *Oak Glen*

*E*lena buttons her white cape against the chill and crosses Taraval Street at dusk. The fall sunset casts its autumnal sky, painting with red and pink and orange hues—a stark contrast to the verdant tree feeling inside Baba and De-doo's log house.

It seems another world outside the house, vibrant and lively. Across the street, restaurants and cafes start to pick up for the evening meal. Groups of teenagers walk a pace slower than she does, breezing in and out between groups of people.

Elena doesn't know how to meander. She walks deliberately, as she always does. Cars travel east and west, stopping at crosswalks where red and green lights cast shadows, illuminating the street, throwing their reflections of color out at stores and restaurants. She surveys the younger people as she passes. Slung on their backs they wear colorful canvas packs with decals and sayings announcing themselves, so different from her red shoulder bag. She considers how much more easily a pack with straps like theirs would hold her acorns.

As she passes they sneak quick looks at her and amongst themselves. Perhaps they're staring at her white cape, the red bag. Certainly they don't hold acorns in their packs. Surely they're carrying books. She's never even gone to school. Instead, Father Al sent her to Baba and De-doo's, saying they would teach her everything she needed to know about life. She never questioned his certitude. Now she begins to wonder what she would say to any of these teenagers if they asked her what she does all day. Butchering or hunting, she might say. Gardening and animal husbandry. She fastens her collar to keep warm and focuses on her feet.

Gathering pounds of acorns at night seems a formidable task. She has a three-and-a-half-mile walk from the Sunset District to the area near the Panhandle where the grove of oaks lives—a dark and secluded section of the park. She reaches into her pocket for solace, trusting her doll to help her, remembering how she was a gift from her mother, who indeed loved her and brought her to safety, as De-doo reminded her tonight.

When she nears Stanyan and Fulton, she enters the wooded area and walks toward Oak Glen. It's the blue hour: her favorite time, when the sun is sinking and its blue wavelengths dominate. It will last thirty or so minutes, giving her time to center herself in the wooded glen before the task ahead.

At her feet, piles and piles of acorns are heaped together among moist dirt and dried oak leaf—a mulch thick with moisture, a soft carpet for her tired feet. She sits on the root of the grandest oak and squeezes her hands into the moist earth stuff, squishing her fingers through to sift for acorns, arousing the sweet and fecund smell of minerals. She pulls up a handful of acorns, smooth and slippery and too tiny to yield enough meal for bread unless she gathers hundreds—thousands, even. It could take more than one night to sift these from the dirt and fill her sack. She wishes Vasilisa were here to help her. It would be fun then.

Baba again and again and again asks her to do impossible tasks.

In a voice only her doll can hear, Elena says, "Please help me, Kukla."

You must begin. Is this a thought, or a mandate from Kukla, or maybe even from Baba?

She hears a sudden, distant roar. Is it a giant wave from the Pacific Ocean, or a wind thrusting boldly from the sea? She listens to what sounds like a whir, a great whisper. The wind stirs from the west, heading toward the grove where she sits. A rustle in the faraway trees becomes a clamor, hastening toward nearby trees until it reaches her. The branches in the canopy whirl, twisting and swirling in some wild dance. Freed by the wind, they sway. The branches tango with each other, brushing closer and farther away, inspired by the great breath of the wind. The canopy of the oaks shimmies and shakes and then she hears, among the whirring music of the wind, loud drops distinctly falling to the ground. At first it's a pitter-patter sound. Acorns. Then what seems like thousands rain down on the earth.

Scared, Elena covers her ears and then protects her head with her arms as the acorns shower her. It's as if a tree spirit is orchestrating a symphony, with the acorns playing the base drum. She listens to the pop-pop-pop and bum-bub-bum and ping-ping-ping. Sheltering herself, she tracks the multiple beats. She counts a full minute of high and low sounds. She bows her head to the rhythmic symphony.

As it quiets, she kneels and closes her hands around the plump acorns—full-bellied ones with smooth skin and pointy tips. Shiny and beautiful, they fill her outstretched hands—some as single crowns, some in pairs, and others grouped into clusters with small caps on top of their heads that remind her of Russian crowns. She grabs fistful after fistful of acorns. The wet fallen leaves feel sharp; their pointy edges pinch her hands as if they resist being disturbed. She begins to place the acorns inside her red bag, where they cling together in the dark bottom with no protective leaves or mulch—alone, but together.

She stuffs handful after handful into her sack, yet it never seems to fill—it just sucks them in, asking for more and more, seeming to have an insatiable appetite that reminds her of Baba.

It seems hours go by. She saw the moon low on the horizon at some point, and now it rises, reflecting on her red bag. For hours she's been filling and filling, yet her bag remains hungry. She keeps gathering, sorting leaves from nuts, until a sweet exhaustion overtakes her and she has to rest. She lies back against the tree and falls asleep, dreaming that the acorns are jumping into her open sack.

Awakened by a howl, Elena sits up. The moon, directly above her now, lights up the midnight sky. The wind has passed. It's still.

Alert, she listens. What did she hear? An owl? A coyote? No, a cry, more human than coyote. She gets up, brushes herself off, and stands quietly for a long moment, looking in the direction of the dull lament. *Pain*, she tells herself. She grabs her bag and slowly moves through the trees toward the moaning; a sliver of moon still visible through the trees lights her way.

She stops. *Here he is again! Oh my God!*

On the ground in front of her lies Frank. She's not surprised. Of anyone in the world she might have encountered in this moment, she realizes Frank is the most likely, since their paths keep crossing in such strange ways.

"You're not okay," she says to him, moving closer. He's holding his stomach, and she sees that his foot is trapped between the fallen limbs of a great tree.

She kneels down beside him. At first he doesn't seem to see her. His eyes are closed and he moans in low prolonged sounds—"oooh, ahhh, oooh"—with each exhalation. She smells something on his breath, a similar scent to the one Father Al has after he sips wine at mass.

Frank opens his eyes and just stares at her for a long moment.

"It's you," he finally says, his brow and upper lip glistening with sweat. "Where am I?"

"I'll help you," she says.

"I recognize this place; it's Oak Glen," he says slowly.

She bends toward where he holds his ankle. On her knees, she clears the mulch and debris from his foot, reminding her of her acorns. Beside her, the sack rests. But then maybe this is part of her task, she reasons. Maybe she was supposed to be here tonight to help Frank.

He doubles over, clutching his stomach. "Just relax your foot," she coaxes. "I know how to do this."

As he relaxes his foot, she gently frees it from the tangle of exposed roots breaking through the soil by jiggling one of the branches. When he's free from the maze, she raises his foot with both her hands and places it gently on a dry log. She sees that the bone is displaced, maybe fractured.

"Wait here," she says. "Don't move." She walks into the thick brush behind him to find a piece of branch to make a splint for his ankle.

She finds the perfect branch. *But what can I use to wrap his ankle?* A cotton half-skirt she wears under her black woolen skirt will do. She takes off the muslin under-skirt and tears it into long strips about five inches wide. She works quickly, worrying that she's been away too long. What if he gets worse? She listens and hears a soft moaning.

She gathers the long strips she just made, then ties the woven material into a knot. With the stick and the muslin in hand, she walks back to Frank.

He looks small, sitting in the dark woods, holding his lower leg and foot in his hands, bent over in pain. She wants to help him.

"I have to make a splint," she says to him, feeling into the mulch beside the log. He nods. She removes his tennis shoe and places the small flat branch she found parallel to his ankle near the large ankle bone.

"Barefoot again," he says with a half-smile. Beads of sweat run down his face.

"Yes," she acknowledges, remembering him standing at the pond, barefoot, and watching her kill the duck.

"It hurts everywhere," he says.

She nods and begins to wrap the white muslin strips around his ankle and around and under his arch. Soon the splint is in place.

"Thank you, Elena." He's speaking so quietly she has to lean in. "I was so supposed to save you," he whispers.

She doesn't know what to make of this proclamation, so she says nothing.

"How'd you know I was here?" he asks.

"I didn't." She too marvels at the coincidence and again thinks about whether Baba knew he'd be here. "I'm here for acorns, that's all."

They sit a moment in the stillness of the urban forest, her red sack by her side.

He clutches at his stomach again.

"What happened to you?"

"Kicked in the stomach. A guy I know from high school." He moans again.

"Let's get you out of here," she says. "You won't be able to bear weight on your foot. Who can we call?"

"My brother," he says, and pulls something from his pocket.

Elena looks at the face of what looks like a rectangular glass case. It's the phone she saw him use in his cab that first day when he waited for Anya.

"Shit!" he says. "There's no service. You'll have to help me get to the clearing."

She's about to go back into the trees to find a sturdy branch he can use as a crutch when she remembers Baba's herbs. She takes the small purse from her pocket and places it beneath his nose. She holds it there, waiting, until his breathing evens out.

When he settles, she goes searching for the branch. It doesn't take long to find a sturdy one. She carries it back to him and helps him to stand.

"Put your weight on my shoulder," she says. He protests, but she stops him. "I can take more of your weight. It's okay. You use this as a crutch on your other side." She hands him the branch she collected.

He gets to standing, leaning heavily on her shoulder. She wraps her arm around his waist.

Luckily, they don't have very far to go. Within a couple of minutes, they have made it out of the woods and onto a path not far from Fulton.

Frank sits down on the path, swipes sweat from his brow with the back of his hand, and then checks his cell.

"Thank God," he says. He dials and asks for Fred. After a pause, he says, "Can you pick me up at the corner of 6th and Fulton? Yeah, I'm okay. An accident, that's all." He looks at Elena, who is standing to his side near the path into the woods. "My brother will be here soon."

Together, they wait. When she sees the car pull up, Elena backs slowly into the woods.

"Hey, wait," Frank calls. "My brother will give you a ride home."

She moves farther into the grove but stops where she can still see and hear him say, "Wait, don't disappear."

She hovers there. Her bag full of acorns seems light as a feather compared to Frank. She watches as a car door opens and a taller, older Frank comes around and helps her Frank into the car.

Once he is safely inside, she answers, "I won't disappear, Frank," and then starts toward home on the wooded path.

A half-hour later, Elena enters the church and finds Father Al kneeling in front of the altar in the chapel. One white candle flickers in an amber votive. His head is bent so far down that his chin rests on his chest and his beard flows over his hands as he prays. She takes in his long, sinewy hands—the same hands that pinned her doll to her shirt when she was an infant; the same hands that made her porridge as a child and stroked the feathers of the dead duck. His hands express kindness.

She quietly walks down the aisle to his kneeling pad and kneels beside him. He acknowledges her but continues to pray.

"Father," she says, "it's so late. You must have been worried."

His soft hum answers, and it has the same calming effect on her as Baba's soporific herbs and Frank's smile. Sounds, almost inaudible, pulse as soft vibrations, mesmerizing her. The quiet of the place puts her in a meditative state. She closes her eyes to the flickering candles and sees her life as a ribbon of many colors: different shades of red—ruby, magenta, carmine—white with gentle yellow and pinks and blues running through; gold that shines like a star flickering in the night sky.

Now a white light comes in through the window; maybe it's the smiling moon signaling its descent.

Finally, Father Al stops his humming and looks at her.

"Child, I have been praying for you."

"We've been praying together, Father Al."

"I pray for your safety."

"I am safe, thank you," she says. She remembers her dream and how Baba appeared in that still-frozen moment—twirling and spinning, generating a spark, obliterating Anya.

"I know you have been doing important tasks," he says. "You have learned well to take care of yourself."

She smiles. "I have my doll, and Baba."

"You are ready for the next passage," he says, placing his hand on her cheek.

"Will you tell me what that is, Father Al?"

"You will move away from Baba's training ground and become closer to people your own age. You will teach and learn from others, expand to meet the life around you."

She thinks of the teenagers she saw this evening, and of Frank. "Will you tell me how Anya is connected to my mother?"

"Anya is a witch who cast a spell on your mother, making her sick. Your mother freed herself by coming to San Francisco so you could be safe and away from the wicked creature. Anya has been searching for you ever since; she wants to kidnap you and take you away from here—to finish exacting her vengeance."

Elena squirms, fear rising, at this ugly thought.

He reaches an arm around her. "Though she creates much havoc, Baba has a plan to strip away her power so we will be rid of her for good."

This part she knows, since De-doo said as much, though she doesn't know *how* Baba will get rid of her. She tells Father Al about meeting Frank again—about finding him in Oak Glen, moaning, and how she made a splint so he could get to the sidewalk and call for help.

The priest is not surprised. "Frank thinks he's protecting you, but it's the other way around, Elena. He means well."

She knows this is true—that she is helping him, and also that they are connected. Frank is a kind person.

"Let us pray for him," Father Al says

He prays aloud, asking God to protect Frank—and Elena too.

Elena reflects on the strange day, and on the notion that she might not see Baba and De-doo again. "Could that be so?" she ponders aloud.

"When they complete their work, they are free to return to their world." Father Al is either reading her mind or understands what she knows, what De-doo told her.

"Their world up north?" she asks.

"Perhaps so."

"And what is their work?"

"To protect you and help you to develop your intuition," he says. "They did the same for me."

"Father, is Baba Vera a witch?" she asks.

"You ask about one of the great questions of life. All I can say for sure is that she dwells in mysteries."

Elena nods her agreement. Baba's clairvoyance, her insatiable appetite, her harvesting of herbs, her broom, her animals, her teachings and tasks—all of it is a mystery to her.

"Remember, we each have a calling," Father Al says, squeezing her hand gently, comforting her. "You can draw upon what you have learned from Baba, but you must mostly rely on your own skills and trust yourself."

"Thank you, Father."

He nods and takes her arm and together they leave the sanctuary: Elena in her white cape, holding a sack of plump acorns, and Father Al wearing his black cassock and hat.

He walks her out toward the vestibule; from there, she ascends the stairs to her attic bedroom. Through her window comes the diffuse light of the twilight before sunrise.

CHAPTER 17: *A Deer in Headlights*

*T*he girl was gone. Disappeared into the forest. Had she really just rescued him? He envisioned himself her protector, and yet when had he ever protected her? He felt some embarrassment. Things were turned around for him: Had there been some switch in intention, or was it all meant to be?

This new awareness—the knowledge that her hands could both kill a duck and save his life—pulsed through him. Didn't she just exhume him from the earth and raise him from the dead? He trembled with a feeling of awe and gratitude. She had unburied him from the wet earth, where he was strangled by undergrowth; fashioned a splint for his ankle; made crutches from a branch; then carried him out of that tangled forest of mulch, twigs, fallen limbs, leaves, and dirt. She'd healed him with herbs. If it hadn't been for her showing up in that way, he wondered whether anyone would have found him, and what state he might have been in by then.

Not for the first time, Frank felt like he was in a fairy tale. The world appeared stranger than he'd ever imagined it could be. He'd assumed she'd let Fred drive her home. *But no, she comes out of nowhere and then disappears the same way.*

"Are you okay? Frank, look at me," Fred said, pulling him away from his thoughts about Elena.

"Pack Taurus kicked the shit out of me at the bar."

"That guy is such an asshole," Fred said. Then he turned to look at Frank square in the eyes. "What the hell were you doing at the bar?"

Frank looked back at his brother blankly.

"Didn't we just have dinner together a few hours ago? And how'd you even end up out here?"

Frank confessed that he'd gone to his old hangout for a beer after their dinner; how he hadn't been thinking straight; how Pack had pummeled him; how he'd lost track of where he was because the pain was so bad; how next thing he knew he'd been caught in the vines at the park. He clutched his stomach. "I think the guy broke some ribs on me." He felt a shooting pain with each breath.

"I'm taking you to the ER," Fred said.

"No, I'm okay. I want to go home."

"You're not okay. We're going to the ER."

Fred immediately changed course for Kaiser Medical Center on Geary, less than a mile away. "I can't believe you ended up alone in the park in the middle of the night after being attacked by Pack," he said, shaking his head.

"I wasn't alone. Elena found me."

"I saw her when I pulled up," Fred said.

Frank sighed with relief. He hadn't imagined her after all. "She manifests herself out of nowhere and then disappears," he said, and then told his brother how she'd shown up, released his foot, and made the splint for him.

"You're a lucky guy," Fred said.

Frank noticed the effort it took him just to speak, so he sat in silence, now grateful they were on the way to the ER. The pain in his abdomen was getting worse. "Pachyderm," he managed.

"Yeah, you got pummeled by a pachyderm—Pack the pachyderm," Fred concurred.

Frank stifled a laugh so he wouldn't burst.

"Remember when he almost killed a kid on the Lowell High School football team?" Fred reminisced.

"Yeah," Frank grunted, "and he got hell for it."

"Hell is what he deserves," Fred said as he pulled up to the front door of the ER. "I have a mind to report this incident to the cops."

Immediately an attendant was there, opening the door. Frank moaned.

"Don't move," said the attendant. "Get a stretcher," he called out. "This man can't walk."

Seconds later, he and another man were easing Frank onto a stretcher, lifting and guiding him. They wheeled past others who were patiently waiting, right on up to the admitting nurse.

"What happened to you?" asked a nurse. She looked at his splint.

"It's my stomach," Frank said.

"I'll get him checked in," Fred said, striding up. "He's my little brother."

They sped past the intake worker into an examining room while Fred registered him, like he was a child. Frank gave a limp wave as he met the physician and nurse who would examine him.

They carefully laid him on the table in the examining room, placing his foot gently up on a raised wedge.

"Ouch!" screamed Frank when the doctor put his hand on his left side. "My ribs."

"Some bruise," the doctor said. "May be rib fractures. Have to check your spleen, too."

"I got kicked."

"By an elephant?"

"You might say."

"Blood pressure and pulse rate rapid, Doctor," the nurse said.

"Let's get a red blood count and then get him down to radiology," the doc said. "I need a chest x-ray and a CAT scan for this—he may be bleeding internally. We'll need to watch him overnight."

Fred popped his head into the room. "We'll be here for some time," the doctor said. "You might want to come back later."

Fred crossed his arms over his chest. "I'll wait."

Just as the sun was rising and after a follow-up scan was taken in the wee hours of what seemed like the longest night of his life, Frank was admitted to the hospital so the blood clot in his ruptured spleen could be monitored; the doctor said they needed to be sure the bleeding had stopped before he could be discharged.

In the hospital, Frank dreamt he heard music, a ghostly round. He was back in the forest, alone, feeling the eeriness that could only come in the fall when the days were on the downslope and the wind squealed through the branches of the giant trees, intersected only by the squeal of an owl. There was a drumbeat—ra-ta-ta-ta—or was it his own heartbeat? His cold feet were caught in a snare. He couldn't get loose. His stomach was on fire. The grim reaper had him in his hands. He opened his eyes. Elena was kneeling beside him in a ghostly white cape.

"Wake up, wake up," she said. "Wake up, Frank."

When he opened his eyes from his dream, Fred was standing beside him.

"Hey, buddy." Fred squeezed his arm. "You were talking in your sleep."

"What did I say?"

"'Wake up, Mr. Cabdriver.'"

A big smile spread across Frank's face, and he closed his eyes. She was the happy face in his dream, just as she had been in the glen. He imagined hearing her say she wouldn't disappear.

He also remembered what he hadn't said to her: *I'm scared here under the night sky with coyotes howling and little slimy creatures in the mulch tickling me. I'm scared. A man is not supposed to be scared. I'd almost given up when you found me.*

He was amazed by her confidence; the way she talked to animals—how even when she had to kill one, she did so with grace. Fear, it seemed, did not exist in this girl's language.

I must stand beside her and learn from her, he thought. *She has something to show me. If I watch and listen carefully, she will.*

He opened his eyes again. "You're still here," he said, feeling grateful for his brother's care.

"No way I'm going to miss these dreams," Fred said, inching closer to the bedside. He waved a small purse in front of Frank's nose. "Did you get this from her too?" He handed him a rectangular pouch filled with herbs. "It was in your trouser pocket. Smells like laurel, and deep licorice from the fields."

"Yes, it's hers." Frank reached for the pouch, brought it to his nose, and sniffed deeply, letting the fragrance open up his senses. Deep, earthy minerals spiced with lighter herbs induced drowsiness. He felt tired; he began to nod off again.

The music came back to him right away—first the drumbeat, then a cry, then the scream, an uncommon pitch. The running. The racing. The frantic searching. Right and left, running up and down. Until the voice said again, "Wake up, wake up, Mr. Cabdriver," and he opened his eyes.

Fred was still there. Frank didn't know if he'd been out one minute or one hour.

"You're okay, buddy, you're okay," Fred reassured him. "They just want to make sure the bleeding stopped. It's the medicine. You'll be home soon."

Just then the doctor entered the room.

"Good morning, Frank," he said. "The CT scan shows your splenic injury is mild and the bleeding has stopped. You're a lucky man."

"Yes, thank you. I didn't know how bad it was." *If she hadn't shown up, what might have happened to me?* He shivered at the thought, not daring to think of being passed out in the park, bleeding internally, in the middle of the night. His heart filled with gratitude for the girl.

"We'd like to keep you here and watch you today, just in case," the doctor said. "You'll need some rest." He looked at Fred, as if asking for assurance.

"You bet," Fred said. "I intend to keep a good watch."

"Today we'll repeat some tests, and if you remain stable—that is, no more bleeding—you'll be out of here tomorrow morning."

"And my foot?" Frank looked down at his foot. "Will I be able to walk?" He was beginning to feel trapped, like a captured animal. And how would he drive his cab, and who would pick up Henry O that morning? Frank had never missed a day before.

I've got to get to a phone to call Henry.

In front of him, the doctor was still talking. ". . . we'll replace the temporary splint we put on last night with a cast this afternoon. By the way somebody did a hell of a job splinting your ankle. Mighty talented, whoever it was."

"Yeah, a fifteen-year-old girl did that." Frank perked up.

"Knew what she was doing, too," the doctor said. "Any chance she wants to go into medicine, have her give us a call." He chuckled. "That said, you do have a fracture, so no, you won't be able to walk right away. A tech will wheel you down to orthopedics to be fitted with a walking cast and crutches today. Try not to bear weight at first."

"What about driving, Doc?"

"No driving," he said, "not for a while. Just rest for now." With that, he left.

Frank looked at Fred. Panic replaced pain.

"But how will I get around—how will I do my job?" he said. He began to sweat and he felt a tight band of pressure at his temples, like his pulse was running wild. *Oh my god, how will I manage?* He didn't want to have Fred miss more work for him. He'd already spent enough time with him. He didn't want to fail his customers, either.

He wanted to flee.

He wanted to see Elena and thank her.

Less than twenty-four hours later, Frank was discharged with a stable splenic injury, a walking cast, and two metal crutches. He walked out the front door of the Geary Street Hospital into the fresh air, where he waited for Fred to pull the car around.

He breathed in the moist San Francisco air, relishing the scent after having been confined in the hospital. He wanted to see Elena and tell her how she had saved his life. He knew where to find her, but he didn't want to ask Fred to take him to her.

Once he was settled in the passenger seat, he said, "Fred, are you free today?"

"Restaurant's closed today," Fred said cheerfully. "Day off. Hungry? We can get takeout at the Cinderella. Get you a Napoleon."

"I want to find Elena. I need to go to thank her. Can you drive me to Taraval Street?" He flashed the pack of dried herbs at Fred.

Fred looked concerned. "You're getting ahead of yourself, buddy."

"It's just . . . I won't be able to rest until I see her. I promise, seeing her will help me rest."

"Where does she hang out? Not in the park all day, I hope."

"No, at a house on Taraval. Maybe we'll find my cab there too. Oh my God, my cab!" He couldn't believe he'd forgotten about it. The real world was setting in again. A hot feeling rose in his body. He imagined his skin all red, as if he were on fire. Not having his cab flooded him with fear. He hated being dependent, a burden. He was sweating and shivering, fire and ice.

"What if I lost the cab? What if it got towed? Or stolen?"

"Whoa, whoa," Fred said, placing a hand on Frank's arm. "Let's go look around the hood for it, then I'll take you to her."

Frank shook his head. "Her first," he said, thinking about the strange-looking narrow house with the workshop storefront and the side passage. How he'd let himself in while he waited to pick up that crazy Russian woman. That was the day this had all started.

"You sure?" Fred asked.

"I'm sure," Frank said firmly. "Take me."

CHAPTER 18: *Left with Tools*

*E*lena walks to Baba's in the first rain of the season, smelling the musky freshness. It was a long night in Oak Glen last night, gathering acorns and helping Frank, but she slept well in her nook and feels rested.

She arrives at the Taraval house around midday, soaking wet. Although her woolen cape seems to repel the beads of rain, the wool sucks up the moisture and weighs heavy on her shoulders. Or maybe the heaviness she feels is about Frank, or about the possibility that Baba and De-doo won't be there. She pats Kukla for assurance. *I hope they're all right.*

She quietly enters the shop. De-doo is nowhere to be found. On his favorite seat he has left a carefully folded note with her name on it; she puts it into her pocket for the time being, to save for after she's had a chance to look around.

She passes through the studio and then the middle room, where she carefully hangs up her cape before unlocking the door to Baba's living space. The house smells of burning wood and sage. Someone built a fire hours ago, and its embers are now sending out their last remains.

Half-expecting Baba to jump down from her bunk, Elena looks around—but it's clear Baba's not there. She exhales deeply, frankly relieved Baba won't be playing tricks on her anymore. She won't miss her jumping out of nowhere to scare her with her boo-hoo-hoos and other rhymes and riddles. And what about those fantastic tasks? She never knew what to expect.

She looks around again—but no, she's really gone. Two of the guinea pigs, White and Red, play with the straw that's strewn all over the floor.

She moves toward the stove to warm herself, thinking about the grinding task ahead of her and wondering whether the acorns could have been damaged by the rain. But no, they thrive in rain, don't they? Didn't she find them in the moist soil? Or maybe they found her, jumped into her sack in the windstorm. She thinks of Frank, who, like the acorns, seemed to grow out of that mulch. How strange to stumble upon him in the oak forest like that—though she knows it was no accident that she was the one to find him. She touches Kukla, feeling gratitude for her steady presence.

She lays the acorns out on several trays, admiring their smooth texture and shiny brown color, sorting them in order of size, lining up the plumpest ones side by side, followed by the thinner ones, then the babies, all so smooth and precious beneath her fingers. She runs her pointer finger over their smooth bodies, aware of their sharp end points. How easy it is today for her to postpone sweeping and tidying up.

She looks around the room one more time, takes in the sound of the guinea pigs chewing on the dried grass and the warmth from the iron stove keeping her company. *Who lit the fire?* she wonders. She looks toward the burning embers. Maybe De-doo did it in the early morning and now he's catching up with Baba.

When she opens the closet for a broom, she once again half-expects to see Baba but only finds her walking stick—about two inches in diameter, made from an oak tree. Elena imagines Baba leaving the house. She would have made a silly ritual of it. Maybe she circled three times around the table, playing ring around the rosie. Elena chuckles at her antics, then picks up the broom and begins to sweep, gathering hay into small piles, making a clean pathway across the center of the room toward the back door and the garden.

The sweeping mesmerizes her, and soon she's lulled into a trance by the swish-swish of bristles and the soft rain on the roof. Like an orchestral hymn, it reminds her of Father Al's chanting last night and the prayer he said for Frank.

As she begins to hum, music fills her heart. She sings along silently, *Oh, lyuli, lyuli, oh lyuli, lyuli.*

Feeling happy, she forgets about the task Baba has given her. As she puts the room in order, she feels her own mind fall into order, too, a relaxing awareness that all is well. She imagines Baba smiling a beatific smile and saying, "Again, you come through for me." Then she notices all the tools that have been set out: grinders she has used to grind pork and beef; hammers, choppers, pliers, and nutcracker; wires and scissors, picks and scoopers; long- and short-handled spatulas and wooden spoons; pots and pans, skillets and huge boilers on the table and floor. They bellow into her calmness, reminding her of the task before her: making acorn flour.

"My work is cut out for me today," she says out loud. "I will start by soaking the seeds." She dumps all the acorns into the five-gallon bucket, knowing she will get through this task as she has the others and that the tools are a parting gift.

She looks at the two guineas, digging in the hay. They're as busy as always. She looks again at the tools set out for her—all familiar. She feels grateful for the skills Baba has taught her.

"I'm pleased to tell you I feel a purpose here," she says to Kukla. "I have been preparing for this moment of being on my own for as long as I can remember." She looks down her chest, making note of her blossoming breasts, acknowledging how she's changing.

"You have all the tools you need." She hears the refrain as if it's her song, her calling. She begins to think the use of tools is her calling.

"Thank you for always being here with me," Elena says. She knows an answer must lie in these tools.

The red guinea pig sits blithely, licking a baking sheet on the floor, while the white guinea rolls itself in the hay. She scans for the black one. He's not there.

Likely Baba took Black, the black guinea who represents darkness. Perhaps she needed the dark for her own journey but left Red, the rising sun, and White, the daylight, for Elena's journey. Her final gifts.

Elena remembers the note she found earlier on De-doo's chair and sits on the lower bunk to read it. Opening it slowly, she runs her fingers over the words in the beautiful Cyrillic cursive, an alphabet she has learned to read from Father Al.

She reads, "My Dear Elena, of course you now know we have left and we are not coming back to Taraval Street. This is your home now. We leave our handsome farm-style cabin to you with affection."

He signed it, "De-Doo Victor."

Tears sting her eyes even as the words calm her. The gift astounds her. This is her house? She closes her eyes and leans into the hay mattress. The prickly spines of hay stimulate her and relax her all at once.

Sleepy, she rests between the red and white guinea pigs, who nestle into her sides after frolicking over her as if they, too, are searching for Black.

Elena falls asleep with the two guineas snuggled beside her, and she stays asleep all that day and through the night, until she wakes up in her new house to someone calling, "Yoohoo . . . yoohoo!"

CHAPTER 19:

The Red One Brings Up the Sun

W hen they reached her street, the cab was not nearby. The place was locked. A sign hung in the window—*Closed for today.*

Frank eased up to the door and knocked.

"Yoohoo," he called. "Yooohooo!"

He heard something—an animal scurrying in the house, a rat maybe—and jumped. "Shit!" He looked at the rooftop, an A-shaped rafter where he suspected hundreds of rats lived. "The place smells like a farm," he said. "Or worse, the zoo." This made him think of how Anya had wanted to go to the zoo.

"Hay?" Fred asked, coming up beside him.

Frank nodded. "It's a weird place," he said.

Then he heard gentle footsteps, almost soundless steps, which he knew belonged to Elena, and from behind the door a soft voice asked, "Who is it?"

"It's Frank," he said.

After a long pause, a key turned and the girl appeared from behind the door. She looked from him to Fred, her eyes asking about the visit.

"Hello . . . umn, umn, umn . . ." He was at a loss for words.

"You're alright." She smiled now, looking at his cast and crutches.

"Yes, thanks to you." He looked down and wiggled his toes. "I wanted to see you, thank you." He took the sachet from his pocket and handed it to her.

"It's for you. I wanted you to have it," she said, looking at his brother.

"Oh, this is my brother, Fred. I can't drive for a while."

He made a funny face and she smiled again. She placed a hand on her pocket, seemed to tap something inside it.

"Would you like to come in for some tea?" she asked.

They followed her toward the rear of the workshop, past the carpenter's workbench and lounge chair. They walked through a middle room and then through another door, leading them across the threshold into a chaotic and strange world.

Frank stopped. The site was paralyzing for him, reminding him of the fight, the screaming between the two women, the curses and threats, and then the vanishing into smoke. His senses overwhelmed him and he didn't know where to look first, so he looked down, where a white animal had just found a spot on his cast. When Frank jumped, the small creature jumped off and joined a red animal of the same size. Guinea pigs. The two animals ran around the living space, disappearing into and then emerging out the back of haystacks, leaving bits of straw littered on the floor.

Lifting his gaze, Frank saw all manner of cooking equipment—grinders, pots, and pans—strewn in disarray. On the wall were weavings and more skulls like the ones outside. A black stove was fired up and gave off an intense heat. A long animal hutch embedded along the far wall of the kitchen was battened down with straw about a foot deep. Candles lit the table.

He stopped at a five-gallon plastic pot filled with plump acorns.

"Acorns," he said, as if they were the common language that would explain everything.

"My grandmother asked me to collect and grind them into a meal for acorn bread," she explained.

Frank only nodded. What a strange girl.

But Fred perked up right away. "Acorn flour?" he asked excitedly." I have a great recipe for acorn flour. Acorn griddlecakes."

"You do?" She looked at him with interest.

"In culinary school I learned how to leach the nuts and then grind them."

Elena was attentive. "Can you help me?" she asked.

"Is that the only stove you have here?" Fred asked, glancing at the black stove and then peeking around the room.

While Fred looked around the space, Frank was looking, too, but it was the hutch that caught his attention. All he wanted to do was to lie down in the hay and sleep. It actually looked appealing, animal smell and all. His eyes felt heavy and he longed to close them. He decided no one would mind if he eased down onto the lower bunk and put his crutches on the floor.

Elena was now showing Fred the black wood-burning stove. "We cook here, and it heats our house too," she said. "You'll be amazed how hot it gets."

She readied the tea while the two of them talked about recipes. Once the tea was ready, they sat at a small, round table, cupping their mugs, while Frank stayed seated on the hay bed, relaxing. He looked down and saw that the white guinea pig was sitting on his cast again; it must be at home with the color, he thought, or perhaps he liked the texture of the plaster.

Elena was suddenly standing next to him, holding a steaming

cup of tea. "You look better," she said, her eyes warm, her free hand resting on her cheek. "It looks like the pain is gone—and now you have a proper cast too." She handed him the tea.

"The doctors were impressed with the splint you made," he told her.

"My grandma taught me," she said. She looked around, as if she expected her grandmother to emerge at any moment. "And your other injury?" she asked.

Frank told her how the stomach injury was more complicated—that his spleen had been injured and he'd been bleeding internally, but it had miraculously stopped. They had watched him overnight, taking several scans, and then they'd released him.

He lifted his shirt, exposing the bruises on his skin. "Broken ribs too."

"I have just the salve for that," she said, and skipped off. Seconds later, she returned with a wet pad that smelled like dung and rotting mint.

"Interesting scent that is," Frank said, coughing into his hand. "Pungent."

"Lie back," Elena said gently.

Frank reclined back onto the hay bed, and she placed the medicinal pad on his ribs.

"There," she said. "That will help."

While Frank, outstretched on the hay mattress, contemplated the effects of the herbs, Fred looked at the five-gallon bucket filled to the brim with shiny acorns and said, "Fresh-fallen acorns are best."

"Oh, yes, they're very fresh," she said, searching Frank's eyes.

"That night's a blur to me," Frank said.

"I'd planned to process the acorns before the morning." Her chin fell and she looked sad. "Well, the truth is, I'd love your help. My grandma's been away. Though she pulled out the tools for me before she left."

"We can help you," Fred said, and he began to explain the multi-step process needed to cure the acorns and to mash them. It seemed an impossible job to Frank, but he had confidence in his brother. He'd just watch and listen, and maybe put his feet up. Right now he was getting a kick out of the white guinea lapping at his toes, and he was enjoying the thickly battened platform of hay; it felt pretty comfortable to him, despite an occasional jab from a pointy piece of grass.

Fred and Elena's conversation was an easy rumble in his ears.

"We'll begin by flooding the acorns in the plastic bucket." Fred got up and filled the plastic pail with water and watched which acorns floated to the surface. "These are the bad ones. They have a corn weevil larvae." He took a scooper from the floor and got rid of them.

"There's always bad ones in a group," Frank said, thinking of Pack Taurus and his violent behavior. At the thought his leg shook, knocking the guinea pig to the floor. He watched it scamper away, then tuned into the conversation again.

"Now let's drain these acorns and place them on baking sheets to dry," Fred said. "Can we put them on low heat? Not too hot for this, just 250 degrees."

Elena showed him a way to bake at a low heat in the iron stove.

When the acorns were dry, Fred began to show Elena how to crack the nuts with the mallet. But she didn't seem to need much help there.

The red guinea pig ran at the sound of the hammer and nuzzled into Frank's side—gently, as if to mend his injury. Frank's eyes were at half-mast, watching Fred working beside Elena. It looked so natural for the two of them.

They cracked all the dried acorn shells, separating the thick skins and the shells from the nuts by rubbing them with their fingertips.

"Now for the leaching process to remove the poisonous tannins," Frank said. "We'll boil them for sixty minutes, then taste them to assure the nuts are no longer bitter." It would take three boils, he explained, and then they'd begin to mash them with the potato masher, three cups at a time. Then they'd spread the mixture on the sheets and low bake it once again.

As they cracked, hammered, and mashed, Frank rested on the bed of hay and listened to the hushed voices of his brother and the girl. It gave him a sweet feeling, and he wondered what it would have been like if he'd had a sister.

"In the morning you can sift it into flour," Fred said, then turned to look at Frank. "Hey, buddy, your eyes are drooping."

"Ready for sleep, that's all," Frank said. "This hay is nice—pretty comfortable. Apart from the occasional jab, that is."

"You can't sleep there; Baba would be mad," Elena said. "But please, before you leave will you give me a recipe for the griddle-cakes in case she returns?" Her voice cracked on the last word.

Fred wrote his Cherokee acorn griddlecake recipe on the back of his card as Frank collected his crutches from the floor and struggled to his feet. But before they left through the middle room and the workshop, Fred asked, "What is that stone sculpture on the wall?"

"Those are bones," Elena said matter-of-factly. "The house protectors."

Frank shivered. "And the guinea pigs? I'm becoming fond of this white one."

"White is the noon sun," she said. "Baba thought of him as her day."

"And the red one?"

"The red one brings up the sun—he was her sunrise," she said.

Frank nodded, satisfied to meet them officially.

They thanked Elena and saw themselves out.

"We gotta find your cab now," Fred said. "It must be on Sacramento, buddy. We'll find it." He patted Frank's leg. "I can see why you think she's special."

Frank nodded, glad that his brother saw what he saw. "Yeah," he said simply. "One of a kind."

CHAPTER 20: *Parade of Fools*

*I*n the late morning, Frank sat on the couch in his apartment, expecting a call from Henry O. When he'd heard about Frank's injuries, he'd offered to drive him around in his own cab that weekend.

Frank, touched, had tried to demur, telling Henry he had his own job to worry about—but Henry had insisted that he had the time. Finally, Frank had agreed—mostly so that Fred wouldn't have to drive him around everywhere. His brother had done enough for him already.

Sleeping in had refreshed him. It had been a long day of watching acorn smashing and grinding with Fred and Elena at the strange log cabin, though resting on the hay bed with that herbal pack had helped. *What were those herbs?* he wondered. He looked around for the smelly poultice Elena had sent him home with. He must have left it in Fred's car.

The phone was ringing. He reached over to pick up his cell. "Hello?"

"Henry O here. I got your cab . . . your brother found it and then picked me up."

"Where was it?"

"Near his restaurant."

Frank suddenly remembered that he'd driven to the bistro from Jane's. Had that really only been a few days ago? His mind was clearing. He'd left his car to walk to the pub after drinking a bottle of wine. That was three days ago now. He remembered, counting backwards from the night at the bar, to the hospital, to the log cabin, and then his house, and now.

He was marveling at his own stupor when he heard Henry say, "Can I come over?"

"I'm here, ready and waiting." Frank was already lonely and dying for company.

"Be there in ten minutes," Henry said.

By the time Frank got down the stairs, Henry was there, getting out and opening the passenger door.

"How the tables have turned," Henry said, chuckling.

"Will I be your first passenger?" Frank asked.

"Nope," he said. "I actually picked up a woman just for fun at the George. She was waving me down like she knew me. Maybe she thought I was you. I stopped. She got in the passenger seat. I think seeing me in the driver's seat shocked her. Once she got over the surprise, she asked me to take her to Our Lady Church."

Weird! Frank thought of Anya, praying it wasn't her. What were the odds it would be her? *One hundred percent*, he told himself. He knew it was her. He listened to Henry go on about how he loved driving the hybrid yellow cab.

"I left my job yesterday," Henry announced. "No more kowtowing to that jackass, prissy boss. I can drink coffee with the girls at the coffee cart whenever I want," he said, "and now I get to drive you around."

"The timing is perfect," Frank said, laughing, but worry hovered in his mind. He wanted to get back to Anya. "Tell me about the woman you picked up."

"A strange woman," Henry said. "Like I said, she was waiting there at the George like she was expecting your cab. Hopped in and looked disappointed that I wasn't you—until she saw this smelly poultice sitting on the seat. She grabbed it and put it right up to her nose."

"Smelly poultice?" Frank lit up.

"Yeah, Fred gave it to me to bring to you. Said it was for your pain." Henry looked around now. "I got it back from her—took it away and put it in the glove box, tucked it into a little purse that seemed to be waiting for it."

Frank reached into to the glove box for the moleskin pouch. Nothing. He shook his head. "No herbs, no purse."

"Oh my God—the nerve of that woman," Henry said. "She must have stolen it. I'm sorry."

It occurred to Frank that Anya now had something that belonged to Elena, something not meant for her hands. He didn't know what about that was so deeply unsettling to him, but he knew Anya was not of this world and that she must have intentionally taken Elena's herbs for some sinister purpose.

"Let's go by Our Lady and try to retrieve it," Henry said. He turned the car toward the church. "She was some cookie. She immediately pulled out a cigarette and a light and started to light up. When I told her she couldn't smoke in the cab, she cussed and hollered. She was wild, like some sort of banshee. My impulse was to stop and tell her to get the hell out of the cab, but I was curious too." Henry caught Frank's eye. "This was a real live case, right here in the car with me. My investigative mind was working."

Frank couldn't help but laugh. "I like your spirit, Henry."

"Just a few more blocks away," Henry announced. "Then let's drive to the Cliff House and get some lunch."

Fred was hungry, but he felt some urgency to find Anya. He had no idea what he'd do if he saw her. It wasn't like he could get out and run after her, wrestle her to the ground, and make her give back his pouch. He couldn't even believe he was thinking about wrestling an old woman to the ground—but then, she was no ordinary old woman.

When they pulled up to the church, everything was quiet. There was no sign of Father Al or of Anya. Henry got out, walked up to the front door, and pulled. It didn't budge. He knocked and waited, mouthing to Frank, "I'll get the damn thing."

Frank watched him knock again and noticed that his anxiety was spiking. What if Anya had already found Elena? Would she hurt her? He squirmed in his seat.

"Nope, no one home—all quiet in there," Henry said, getting back into the driver's seat.

"Okay," Frank said, feeling disturbed but not knowing what to do. "To the Cliff House, I guess . . . I'm hungry."

Henry started driving the twenty blocks west to the ocean.

And then—there she was. Frank couldn't believe the serendipity of it. Anya was running along the street, at a pace that seemed far beyond the capacity of someone her age. They were just a block away from the Cliff House now, at the parking lot near the Sutro Bath ruins. Henry parked and she ran right past them, not seeing them, toward the rustic stairs leading down to the old baths and then the breakwater that had once protected the massive pools from the surging sea.

Crashing waves pounded on and over the wall. Anya was a flurry of activity, screaming, her hair flying in all directions, clutching her floral purse in front of her, a cigarette dangling from her lips; she was acting as if someone were after her, or like she had some important meeting.

"Have you ever seen anything like it?" Henry asked, quickly

turning off the car and throwing the door open. "I'm getting that pouch!" He jumped out of the car and ran down the rough-hewn path after her, dead set on reaching her.

"Wait, someone's chasing her," Frank said—more to himself at that point, since Henry was long gone. He opened the passenger door, balanced on one foot, and scrambled for his crutches.

Frank couldn't believe it. First Anya, then Henry, and now, not more than twenty yards behind, was the scrawny little woman in a short skirt and striped knee-highs, carrying a broom. It was the woman who lived on Taraval—Elena's grandmother, or at least that's what Elena called her. And following her was the tiny round man in a flannel shirt and woolen pants who'd let Frank use the bathroom that day. Was this some kind of mirage?

Standing upright on his crutches, Frank followed the parade of fools down the maintained park service steps. Now he was one of them in the line on the stairs, hobbling along slowly. He no longer could see Henry.

He stopped on the last of the rough-hewn steps, looking for Henry on the slick rocks between him and the sea. What he saw instead was Elena, two hundred yards below, running on the wall on the opposite side of the baths toward Anya.

"There's the girl!" Frank yelled into the air without a hope of being heard by anyone, given the strong winds and the crashing water. He stopped and stared, feeling helpless as his premonition unfolded in real time. Anya was after Elena, and she intended to hurt her. He felt sick in his helplessness.

Frank watched from the sea wall as Anya sped toward Elena. All he could do was take in the scene. Thoughts fired into his brain in the form of a hundred questions: What the hell was Elena doing there? Shouldn't she be back at the Taraval house with her acorn flour? What in the world would have lured Elena into coming here? And what was she carrying? He strained to get a better look and was startled to realize it was one of the skulls he'd seen on the wall of the Taraval house.

Henry was still pursuing Anya on the impossible terrain while the old couple ran behind him—only they were too fast, just like Anya had been too fast. Frank watched in awe as they easily overtook Henry. They looked like they were puddle jumping—and then they were in the air, no longer a couple of wiry old folks but a pair of strange-looking birds, twirling in the air.

Frank rubbed at his eyes, not sure he could believe what he was seeing.

Just as the birds flew over Henry, he tripped on the rocky path, fell forward, and landed facedown.

Frank gasped—then screwed up his courage and headed out onto the rocks. "I'm coming!" he shouted, as if Henry could hear him.

Taking each step was slower than slow for Frank with his cast and crutches. Slipping and sliding on the wet rocks nearer to the pools scared him. After a few steps he stopped, not able to negotiate the final rough path where the old pilings jutted up against the wall.

He squinted his eyes to see the parade of fools reaching the cliff edge downhill from where he stood. Large waves crashed over the sea wall. Anya reached the center of the wall from one direction, while Elena arrived from the opposite direction. What were they doing? They seemed to be walking toward each other, almost like a standoff in a western movie.

Frank tensed with fear as the two met at the middle of the wall and Anya lunged at Elena, hands outstretched as if to get a hold of her neck—but Elena just stood there calmly, holding the skull out like a talisman. Elena pushed the thing into Anya just as the two strange birds shot through the sky just above them, twirling and spinning. A spark flew—and before Frank even understood that the two events must be connected, the skull was aflame and Anya was dissolving. Within seconds, all that was left was a pink cloud.

Frank stood with his mouth hanging open. Millions of feelings crisscrossed his mind. This was the second time he'd seen Anya—now he knew it must have been her the last time—dissolve. Was the first event a prelude? Now there was no denying she was gone.

Every feeling inside him activated simultaneously. "Yes, Elena!" he shouted. "You're free—she's gone!" He felt elated, like a balloon ready to take off.

When Frank looked again, the couple from the Taraval house looked to be gliding into the thin air. There was a spark of light and then they were gone—disappeared. He could swear he heard the old woman say, "Now, dearie, do it cheery," and the old man saying, "Goodbye, love." But of course he was too far away to have actually heard that.

He blinked his eyes to focus on Elena, who was waving goodbye. He watched her, still holding the skull, walk the full length of the wall toward the rough ruins and then up towards Land's End, where she turned into the trees and disappeared into the canopy of windswept pines, never once acknowledging his presence. Was it possible she hadn't seen him?

Henry was limping up the craggy hill, getting back to where Frank was standing at the bottom of the long stairway. Blood stained his khakis. His chin was bruised from his fall. When he reached Frank at the lower end of the stairs, they looked at each other in disbelief.

"Did you just see what I saw?" Frank asked. "Or am I going mad?"

"Yup," Henry said, "that Russian woman just got away. I fell and never caught up with her. Where in hell did she go?"

"You didn't see the spark? Or her dissolving into a cloud?"

"No, nothing like that, my friend," Henry said, eyebrows raised. "She just got away. I couldn't see her once she got over the seawall. Do you think she might have jumped?"

"What about the rest of it?" Frank asked, astonished. "Did you see the girl and the little couple?" He stared out at the horizon.

"I don't know about any of that," Henry said. "I was just trying to get the pouch and I couldn't reach her. I'm sorry. I know you wanted it back."

"But a little couple—a man and a woman—they were running after her, and then they jumped right over you, right before you fell. You saw that, right?"

"I didn't," Henry said. "But you know, I was out for a bit. It was a hard fall."

Frank was dismayed. Was he really the only one who'd witnessed everything? "Weird shit, all of it," he said.

Henry clapped a hand on his shoulder. "You can say that again."

CHAPTER 21:

The Warmth of the Ancestors

After making the acorn flour with Fred, she's tempted to spend the night again at Taraval, but she knows Father Al would worry. So instead Elena finds herself doing the round trip to and from the church in the span of twelve hours.

When she arrives at Taraval Street the next morning, it's quiet. She enters through the workshop and notices that De-doo hasn't laid out his workbench for the morning. She forces herself to remember that they're really gone. She kisses De-doo's armchair where he so often rested his head and locks up his workshop, saying a silent goodbye to her godparent guide. She feels certain she will never see them again. Yet she knows she still must fulfill Baba's plans for her and make the acorn flour, so she walks through the middle room to the kitchen.

The door to the main sanctum of the home opens easily. The embers from the fire they used to leach the nuts last night are cool, but otherwise there is little evidence of the evening's flour-making extravaganza. The place is swept clean. The pots and pans, the sheets for baking, the grinders, the hammers, and the mallets are put away. No evidence of her sorting and cracking and boiling and baking with the brothers last night remains. She is on her own, and she begins to let that sink in.

She cleaned well last night. The hutch lies stacked with a foot of hay, but the red and white guineas are not inside. The last time she saw them was last night, when they were sleeping next to Frank.

She sets to work finishing the acorn flour, sifting the dried mash she and Fred made last night. Soon, her last task from Baba will be done.

The flour is done. Elena cleans up the mess and sets the kitchen in order, then twirls around the empty floor. Baba's broom is gone; the stove is cool. She spins and spins, making herself tall and short, open and closed, feeling her body's freedom, like when she and Vasilisa played spinning as kids.

She looks up at one of the skulls on the wall. It seems to gleam at her, to beckon her. She shivers, though its energy brings her comfort.

"Why you?" she asks. "Do you mean to speak to me on Baba's behalf?"

The skull seems to smile, glowing as if a warm ember sits inside it.

Is there yet another task you have for me?

Yes! The skull doesn't speak it, but Elena intuits its message. The skull has something for her that she must follow.

She jumps up onto the roof of the hutch structure, stretches to her full height, and reaches for the skull. On tiptoes she touches its jaw, inserts her fingers as she used to as a child, and lifts it off its hook.

Once she has it in her hands, she rubs it with her fingers. The bone warms her as if it were alive. She traces the contours of the head and knows that it was a woman.

"Who are you?" she asks.

I am your messenger, she hears.

"I don't understand," she says, but the skull only glows.

Elena trusts this mystery; she waits to know what to do next.

She jumps down from the roof of the hutch, places the bowl of acorn flour inside the skull, and then puts the skull inside her red sack.

"Show me," she says, cradling the sack with both hands. Leaving the kitchen from the side passage, she continues down the passageway to the street.

She walks to Golden Gate Park this way, carrying her red sack with the sifted acorn flour inside the warm skull. In the park, she stops at the lake where the duck family lives and sits in silence, watching for a while, as a white egret dives so peacefully, slapping its wings against the water and stretching its neck like a queen. Elena smiles and wonders if the bird ever thinks about her missing elders.

She picks a blade of grass to feed her doll, who is very still. "Dear Kukla," she says, "I know now what I must do."

The doll's stillness means everything is as it should be.

"I must trust," Elena says, sitting a moment longer, waiting. A duck waddles out of the water and comes to her side. She stops and looks at Elena, trusting her. *Thank you.* Her heart lifts in the bird's presence.

She buttons her cape against the autumnal air, pats the sack, and feels that it's warm to the touch. She puts her fingers into the sack, pulls up a pinch of acorn dust, and puts it to her mouth. As soon as she does, she feels what she must do next: head toward the open ocean. She trusts this thought.

Inspired, she walks quickly down JFK Drive toward Ocean Beach. From there she walks up the hill toward the Cliff House. When she reaches Louis', a café just above the Cliff House, she removes the warm skull from her red bag, removes the bowl of flour, and puts the bowl back inside the bag, knowing the skull alone is her guide to finish what Anya has put into action.

Holding the warm skull near her heart, she takes a side dirt path toward the Old Sutro Baths.

Just as she gets to the breakers, she sees the strangest sight: a strange-looking woman, carrying a floral bag, running in Elena's direction on the rock pier in front of her. She immediately knows it's Anya. Behind her, as if in chase, are two wild-looking, long-necked birds—colorful birds, one of which has red and white stripes on its underbelly. She knows they are Baba and De-doo. It's a great comfort to find them here. She wonders, *Is this a final test?*

Without thinking, Elena rushes toward the woman. They meet on the rocky path, and Elena stares into her savage and crazy eyes. She is uglier than she imagined.

Anya dives at Elena, grabbing for her neck, screaming feral sounds. Indecipherable, and yet they have a strangely familiar cadence to them; they remind her of a song of dark magic in a fairy tale book she once read—a kind of abracadabra, hocus-pocus, and zi-ki-tee-doo clacking sound all rolled into one. What is she saying to her?

Elena pushes the skull, growing ever hotter in her hands, into Anya's face. When it touches Anya, sparks fly out and set fire to Anya's hair, head, and neck, sending ashes onto the sea wall, until *poof*—all that's left is a pink cloud.

Elena looks up. Baba and De-doo, in the form of those strange-looking birds, pass above her, twirling and cawing joyously, waving their long necks. She looks down. The radiant skull sits on the sea wall, cooling down. She picks it up and puts it back in her sack to keep the flour warm, and as she does she hears a familiar love song: Baba chanting, "Now, dearie, do it cheery," and Victor saying, "Goodbye, love."

Elena bows deeply to her guardians, then turns and walks along the sea wall, continuing in the same direction as before.

At the other side, she walks up the uneven path toward the windswept forest of weirdly shaped pines at Land's End—the end of the land before the sea.

On her way home, Elena returns to the duck pond, where she sits in contemplation beside her duck friends, catching her bearings. The acorn flour and the skull rest in her sack beside her.

The cry of a lone coyote who lives in the park is her signal to be on her way to Our Lady. Listening to the coyote's deep cries into the night, she hopes he'll find his clan.

When she reaches home, Father Al is waiting—kneeling next to the altar in prayer, as usual. She kneels beside him and listens to his steady breathing.

For a long time he prays, until, with midnight eyes, he raises his head and looks at her. "I didn't hear you come in," he says.

"You have been praying."

"Yes, for them."

"They're gone. Father Al, do you know where they are?" she asks, though she knows they are spirits now. She watched them fly away joyously. They said their final goodbyes.

"Yes, child, they have returned to their home. They have completed their tasks in this world. They taught you all you needed to know, and they broke the spell."

"Yes, Anya is gone—dissolved into smoke." Elena feels a light within, now freed of the awful woman. "And now what, dear father?"

"You have all the tools," he says.

She looks around the darkened sanctuary. She removes the skull from her pack and hands it to Father Al, who is still kneeling before the altar. It seems to glow pink light for them. He looks at the skull deeply, takes it in his hands, rubs it against his cheek. He confirms that it's the skull of a woman.

"Do you know her, Father?" Elena asks, knowing she is a protective force, a member of his lineage, maybe even his mother.

Tears fall from his eyes and land on the skull's surface. "She is a loved one whom I lost long ago. An ancestor." When he stops crying he gets up, turns to Elena, and places the warm skull in her hands.

"No, Father, the skull is for you," she says. Then she reaches into her pocket and pulls out the key to the Taraval house. "Father Al, De-doo Victor has given me the Taraval house. Will you keep this key for me until I am ready?"

He nods.

He kneels again and soon his chanting fills the room. Elena hums with him in the soft light of the glowing skull. She prays with him for Baba Vera and De-doo Victor, and even for Anya.

Before leaving the chapel, she bends toward the priest and whispers, "Father, I have so many dreams, but I don't know which one is mine." It sounds like a song to her—maybe one she's heard before. "Which one is right for me?" she asks.

"It's all a dream; they are all the right ones for you," he says, pressing his cheek against hers.

Together, they cry, their tears rolling from their eyes and mixing together.

CHAPTER 22: *Fresh New Eyes*

He couldn't sleep; he spent all night tossing in his bed, sorting through the series of bizarre images he'd seen that day at Sutro Baths: the skull in Elena's hands, the old couple outrunning Henry O, Anya disappearing in a puff of smoke.

He peeked out from his blanket. It was still dark in his room, and he knew Fred had already left for the restaurant—the coming holiday meant there was much prep work to do.

The images running through Frank's mind haunted him, and yet seeing the girl holding the skull of fire at the water's edge had thrilled him. He had begun to think of Elena as a gift, rather than as a person he was meant to protect. Clearly he was meant to learn from her.

Convinced that her life's energy intertwining with his mattered, he resolved to talk to her again, though he worried she might think he was stalking her. But he had seen what she had seen, he was sure of it, and Henry O had not, and that had to mean something, didn't it?

She was remarkable—how easily she had killed the duck; how easily she'd shown up to save his life; how easily she'd defeated Anya. One question still tugged at him, however: How had she and Anya both appeared at Sutro Baths at the same time? Was it just fate? Had Anya arranged for it? Had Elena anticipated it? Frank wondered if that smelly pouch Anya stole from the cab had somehow called to Elena, or if the little couple had orchestrated the whole thing.

He played the scene over in his mind in slow motion, not only in disbelief and awe but also with joy. He knew the witch Anya was gone and that the godparents who chased Anya had lit a spark and then lifted off. He'd seen them transformed into crazy-looking birds.

Elena's intimate involvement with this parade of characters still had him confused; it was as if he were falling into a rabbit hole and couldn't catch his fall. He was deep into the mystery now, and he was sure he had a part in it—that he was not just a bystander but a participant.

When he tried to get up, his cast snagged his blanket, reminding him that he was still in a mess—the broken ankle and internal bleeding. He needed to slow it down so he could think straight. He had to calm himself.

He called Jane, hoping she'd pick up. It was still early. He thought about their walk together to the pond, the story of the butterflies and the new cells, the salamanders that had touched him so deeply. He wanted to see her—to process this experience with someone who would understand.

"Frank Hudson," she answered on the second ring. "You finally call." Her voice was welcoming.

"I really could use a talk with you," he said. "Can I come to Marin?"

"Yes, I'm around all day today," she said. "How about two o'clock?"

"Yes, yes," he said.

"Be there, see you."

As soon as he hung up, he called Henry O for a ride. Henry didn't hesitate at the request.

"Great," he said, "gives me a chance to try that new Mexican place in Mill Valley, La Playa."

Henry showed up an hour later. The cab was dazzling in the sun—all washed, maybe even waxed. Frank squinted at his shiny yellow sanctuary like it was a noon sun.

"For you, monsieur." Henry opened the passenger door for Frank and made a half bow.

"Come on, man, get out of here." Frank was embarrassed by the gesture. No one had ever bowed to him.

"Hey, you deserve the best," Henry said as he ushered Frank inside the cab. "You gave me a new lease on life. I resigned from my job because of you; our chats recently got me thinking about what I really want to do. It's an honor to drive you to Mill Valley today." With that, Henry shut Frank's door, scurried around to the driver's side, and got in behind the wheel.

Frank felt lighter, like a new man, as Henry drove them across the bridge. No carrying his bike down the stairs under the north tower this time. He rolled the windows down and wriggled his toes, grateful for the ankle cast that left his toes free to feel the moist air—it was almost like being on his bike.

As they got closer to Jane's, large redwoods guarded each side of the curving road. Frank let out a big exhale. In this enchanted forest, he felt peaceful.

"It should be the next right," he said, grateful for the silence.

Henry wound his way deeper into the canyon. The shade made day turn into shadow, reminding Frank of the mystery surrounding Elena. Soon, the sign for the retreat center appeared.

This, his third visit to these wooded lanes, gave Frank the same magical feelings they had the first time. He breathed in the scents of the wooded refuge, appreciating first the wildness of the redwood trees and then the well-tended, heart-shaped lawn at the center of the circular drive.

Henry stopped the car in front of the stairs that ascended to the magnificent house's front porch, near the handrail. "Some pad," he said. "Give me a call when you want me to come pick you up."

Frank nodded and the two friends gave each other a little fist bump before Frank got out of the car and Henry pulled away.

After making his way up the steps, Frank surveyed the various stuffed chairs and sofas on the porch, landing his eyes on the rocker where a Maine Coon stretched out in what looked like contentment. In his next life, he decided, he wanted to be a cat. He glanced around but Mutter, the dog, was nowhere to be found.

When he turned to the front door, Jane was already standing there, watching him. "Willy's the boss here," she said. "Pushes Mutter out of the picture." She looked at Frank's casted ankle. "What happened to you?"

"I ran into a nasty bull," he said. "And got caught in some roots."

"Ouch!" she said. "Shall we sit here on the porch?"

He nodded and moved toward the sofa they'd sat in the last time he visited.

"How did the roots get you?" Jane asked as she settled into her spot on the couch.

Frank shrugged. "I was cutting across some boyhood terrain and got tangled up."

"No longer a boy," she said. "And the bull?"

"An old bully from high school days," he said. "Tried to kill me."

"You got free."

"Saved by a forest sprite." He winked at her.

"Exciting!" Jane said.

Frank told her everything that had happened the night Pack Taurus pummeled him.

When he was done, Jane asked, "So what made you call me?"

"To tell you what I've seen over the past few days. Can't say which part is real." He looked at Jane. "It feels more like an amazing dream," he said. "*I* feel like a dream being, and then I think *she's* a dream being."

"So you're both dream beings?"

"Yes," he said.

"But what if it's all a dream we live in? Who's to say?" Jane smiled. "Stay in that dream a bit. See where it takes you."

He nodded. Her words supported his experience. "Something about her intrigues me," he confessed. "She's ethereal. She seems like air to me but then she's earthy, too. You know, she carried me to safety." His voice choked up. "Yeah, Elena knows the ins and outs of the ponds and forests of Golden Gate Park as well as I do . . . cares about the same things I do. I admire her and feel a kinship with her. It's like we're on the same path."

"She sounds like your equal in many ways, Frank."

"But she has this uncanny sense, almost as if she's a magician. The night she saved me, the acorns . . ." Frank stopped talking and twisted his hands, pulling his fingers. He felt a joint pop.

"What about the acorns?"

Frank wasn't sure how to explain. "She found me because she was there to collect acorns."

"Hmm!" Jane came closer to him, resting her hand on his arm, easing his discomfort.

"While she ministered to me, her red sack mysteriously filled up with them—more than a bag its size should hold."

"Nature is magical," she said.

He wanted more; he felt his facial muscles twitching as he repeated, "Magical."

"When we witness that magic, it's transformational."

"I never thought of nature as magical until now," Frank admitted. "How everything has a rhythm; how one thing seems to flow into another like a river. I want to trust this magic, but it's just too bizarre! I feel like I'm in a Harry Potter movie."

"The two of you are in sync," Jane said. "It's not an accident. There's a prescient, knowing sense that we can tap into at times. In one moment, clarity arrives—and yes, it seems like magic."

His eyebrows lifted. "That's what I was thinking. It feels like that . . . the way we're on the same path and we're helping each other to grow into ourselves." Picking up steam, he told her about the strange incident at Sutro Baths, the chase, and how he had witnessed Anya dissolve into pink smoke and Elena's godparents turn into birds and fly away.

He expected her to laugh or balk, but she just leveled her gaze at him and said, "Wow."

"I thought I was going crazy—but it was so real, Jane. She dissolved in front of my eyes and the old couple turned into birds and flew away."

"Energy can transform," she said. "I've heard of such things in esoteric Buddhism."

Hearing this explanation, he felt somewhat relieved.

"I was thinking about doing a silent retreat," he told her, "just to get clear, to give myself some space to see who I am and to trust my true nature."

"Let's walk to the pond," she suggested. "You can tell me more about what you want." She looked at his cast, his crutches. "Can you walk on uneven ground?"

"I've been doing that all my life," he said, then laughed at his own joke.

He was grateful to be here again in Jane's presence. He thought she was the most beautiful woman he had ever seen.

Together, they walked under the natural arbor of tall trees. The pond was still. Frank went to the edge, allowing his eyes to acclimate to the world beneath the surface water. Soon the bulging-eyed rowing insects swam toward his shadow and the tadpoles made their appearance. They stopped him in his tracks.

"Are tadpoles the same as pollywogs?" he asked.

"Look down under layers and layers," Jane said. "They're still underwater creatures."

He watched them swimming through the murky water and grasses of the pond. They were tails swishing about, little tails with heads that would eventually grow legs and arms and become frogs. Transform, just like Elena's godparents had done. Maybe Jane was right: energy transformed.

He stood frozen to the spot—not frozen as in cold, but frozen as in all the molecules in his body seemed to be shifting. He heard light splashes in the water and looked down. Beneath him, a whole team of pollywogs had gathered as if conferring over something. He bent his head over the pond and saw his own reflection. His eyes—dark, glassy globes with white and green flecks of light—startled him. Around his nose, ears, and mouth the tadpoles swam, swishing their tails as if entering into his deep crevices—as if he, too, were one of them, a creature yet undeveloped, a creature who would soon transform and find a new way of breathing.

He noticed he was shaking. For a moment he felt slimy and damp, like a water creature. He felt little bodies trespassing into him, tickling his nostrils. He wanted to both pull his head up and shake them off and to immerse himself into the pond.

"Astounding!" Jane said, steadying his arm, which was wobbling on his crutches.

He shook himself to wake up. He'd forgotten she was standing beside him; that he was balancing on two crutches at the edge of the pond; that she had walked with him to see the tadpoles; that she was helping him navigate tough terrain. He'd forgotten he was on crutches with a bum ankle.

"I was imagining being a pollywog," he told her, shaking his head.

"And then transforming into a frog prince," she said, laughing.

"Yeah! Something like that."

She had it right. Frank was thinking about transforming. The time had come, and Elena was some sort of catalyst.

He didn't know what would happen from here, but he knew his life had changed irrevocably. He'd always been the younger brother living with his bigger, more confident and competent brother, but now he was at some kind of threshold. He knew he was meant to see Anya set aflame, and the couple flying away gleefully. And he knew that having been a witness to these phenomenal events, his life would change, as would Elena's. But he didn't yet know how all of this would come about.

He looked into the water again. The deeper he searched, the more he discovered. He saw all manner of vegetation and feeders upon them. The pollywogs had scattered. Were they doing their work now of growing arms and legs?

"The deeper part of one's mind, the one not on the surface but underneath, the one that knows, lives in the cycles of life," Jane said.

What was happening to him felt new and exciting. He had been numb in some way to these sensations until now. Something miraculous was happening to him.

"Frank, do you believe in magic?" she asked.

"Like fairy tales?"

"Like—did you believe in Santa Claus?"

"Of course I did. I still do!" He grinned.

"Sometimes the magical is as true as reality."

"Truer," he said, nodding.

They walked up the path to the stone bridge, as they had done the previous time, only this time it was a slow go. Frank's arms were burning by the time they reached the great stone bench. They sat down to rest.

He listened as the gentle wind sang its awesome song, the ravens accompanying it.

"Is this magic?" he asked.

"I'd say so," Jane said. "Listen to the soundscape."

He heard the sounds of jays and crows and tiny birds singing—a symphony of sounds. A gentle breeze caressed his face. Time quieted for him and he relaxed. He closed his eyes.

When he opened his eyes, the sun was lower.

"You were meditating," Jane said. "Your first Zazan. Just sitting. No thinking mind."

"That was so lovely," he said. Again he turned back to the topic of the silent retreat. "I'm ready to look at myself, and the mysteries of life. I'm thinking about doing something epic, like walking the Camino de Santiago in Spain." He looked down at his cast. "That is, after my foot heals."

"That's a great idea," Jane said.

"Can you recommend a spiritual teacher to guide me until then?"

"I'll be leading a two-week silent retreat with some other teachers in Myanmar in January," she said. "Why don't you start slowly for now, with a daily meditation practice, and then join us for the retreat?"

Frank had all kind of questions, but he simply nodded and said, "Okay."

Back on the porch, Jane gave him a list of San Francisco practitioners for his beginning practice, recommending two younger male teachers in particular that she thought he'd like.

Frank dialed Henry O to pick him up. As he sat and waited, the cat rubbed against his leg, sniffing at his cast and the toes that peeped out.

CHAPTER 23: *Cold Storage*

*E*arly in the morning, Elena wakes in her attic bedroom feeling refreshed at the prospect of a new day. Resolved to bring the acorn flour to Fred's restaurant—the address is on the card he wrote his griddlecake recipe on—she readies herself, kisses Father Al goodbye, and walks to the bistro.

The restaurant is on Sacramento Street near Presidio Avenue, in the opposite direction of Taraval Street, where she's walked every weekday for seven years—ever since she was eight years old.

When she reaches the restaurant, she goes around the back and stops at the door she's certain leads to the kitchen. Before she knocks she puts her ear to the wooden door and hears a low rumble of voices of varied pitch, kind of like a song. She smells a sweet celery-onion-carrot stock, maybe for chicken soup, and she feels the warmth through the edges of the door.

She knocks. A moment later, Fred opens the door.

"Elena," he says.

"Hi, Fred," she says shyly. "Here's the acorn flour. My grandmother won't be needing it." She hands the bowl to Fred.

"Thank you," he says, accepting the gift. "Would you like to help me today? We're doing prep work for the holiday."

"Yes, of course," she says.

He beckons her inside and she follows him deeper into the white kitchen, where large ovens, stainless steel sinks, and butcher blocks line the space. Overhead pots and pans hang on a rack from the ceiling—all sizes of pots, pans, and ladles. Not so different from Baba's utensils, even a collection of fine knives for paring and carving different cuts of meat. She feels at home here.

Fred places the acorn flour in a small fridge. "Maya and Rudolph will help you get familiar with the place." He gestures to a girl sitting on a stool with pigtails and acorn-colored skin, wearing the prettiest cotton top with circular patterns over jeans. A tall boy stands like an oak tree behind Maya, filling a bucket from a bin with red apples. His curly dark hair covers one side of his forehead and falls over one eye. He smiles.

"This is Elena," Fred tells the young people.

Elena imagines they're a little older than she is—probably almost done with high school, maybe in college.

Maya smiles and gestures for her to come sit near her. Elena obeys, and as she sits, inhales a whiff of cinnamon bark. Maya scoops pumpkin from the baked skins, and ears of fresh corn are piled in front of her.

"Your cape is cool," she says. "The aprons are by the fridge."

Elena takes the hint; she rises, removes her cape, and dons one of the aprons hanging on a hook next to the fridge. She hangs her cape there and returns to her stool, awaiting instruction.

Maya moves the ears of corn toward Elena. "Can you shuck these?"

Elena nods and reaches for an ear.

Rudolph carries the tub of shiny apples over and places it next to Elena's station. He smells like the forest after the first rain—woodsy and earthy. Of tannins, too, like Father Al's communion wine.

He shakes his mane of hair from his eyes and nods to her. "Apple pie," he says, looking at the apples. He sits next to her, takes a peeler, and swiftly removes the skin of an apple in one long peel, going round and round in a spiral.

"Fred's making a great sweet potato stuffing with fresh pecans," Maya tells Elena, pointing to a pile of shiny, skinned brown nuts.

"Not so different from cracking the acorns," Fred says.

"Do you live around here?" Rudolph asks. "Do you go to Washington High?"

"No," Elena says, her chin pointed down toward the corn. She peels the silk threads off the corn, watching how they glisten in the sunlight that enters the kitchen through a high side window.

"Ru and I are seniors at Washington," Maya tells her. "Do you go to private school?"

Elena looks toward Fred, who is ladling soup; she doesn't know how to answer. He nods.

"I'm . . . home-schooled," she says, which is neither wholly true nor wholly a lie. She feels awkward, out of her element. She picks up another ear of corn and pulls off the layers of shining blonde hairs as fine as her own hair, as fine as Kukla's little tuft. She hears the tap of crutches and looks up to find Frank in front of her.

"You're just in time," Fred says, nodding.

"Elena." Frank smiles from ear to ear.

"Hi Frank," she says softly, a big smile opening her face. She feels a closeness to him knowing he witnessed what happened at the Sutro Baths yesterday.

"Maya, Rudolph, this is my brother, Frank," Fred tells the high school kids, and then he sets him to work.

"I came by to leave the acorn flour," Elena tells Frank, who's looking a bit bewildered. "Fred asked me to help with the prep work for the holiday."

"Good idea," Frank says. "I love that you're here in our family restaurant."

Before Elena can say another word, Fred directs his brother to the walk-in fridge to retrieve a turkey.

A few minutes later, when Frank hasn't returned, Fred says, "Will you help him, Elena?"

She walks to the far end of the kitchen entrance and comes to a large storage fridge. The door is open. She stands outside and peeps into a dark space, feels the chilled air. Boxes she can hardly make out line the shelves. As her eyes accommodate to the dark, she identifies brussels sprouts, little gems, kale, chard, spinach. The scents of green sweeten the cold air. She inhales deeply and smells freshly cut meats as well—legs of lamb and beef, all familiar to her. She eyes the feet of a freshly killed duck that stick out of one carton.

"May I come in?" she asks, peering into the cold, dark storage room.

"Yeah, flick on the light, will you?" Frank says.

She does, and sees him standing precariously on his crutches in the far corner, shaking in the cold. "Fred thought you might need help."

"I do," he says. "Keep the door open—fridge safety!"

As Elena comes deeper into the cold world, she wishes she'd kept her cape on under her apron. She and Frank look at each other. She marvels at all the ways their lives have intertwined, feels a kind of intimacy with him. Is he like a brother?

She walks up beside him and touches him on his arm. It's cold. "We keep connecting," she says, smiling.

He nods and smiles. She remembers back to the first day of Anya's arrival at Our Lady and then the last day, yesterday, when she disappeared in a cloud of smoke. Elena's eyes connect with Frank's. She wonders what he saw—and whether he believes what he saw to be true.

"I saw you at Sutro Baths," he says, as if reading her mind. "With the skull."

"Anya's gone now."

"Yes, and you're safe."

"I carried the spark that set her on fire," she says.

"You were phenomenal," he says.

"The turkey is on the middle shelf," she says. She's not quite sure how to take the compliment; she only knows that he has been a witness, if not a participant, in her final initiation. She gets up on a wooden stepladder and grasps the large aluminum pot the turkey is in. It's soaking in brine, its legs up in the cold air.

"Your godparents are gone too," he says.

She releases the pan and turns to look at him. "Yes, you saw them leave too." She smiles, thinking of the two birds happily singing their words of wisdom from above. She feels joy at their release—and sadness, too.

Seeming to sense that sadness, Frank says, "You're family now. Me and Fred are here for you."

"Thank you," she says, a curious tickle in her tummy springing forth. "I never had a brother or a sister. And maybe you could use a sister in the family?" She smiles at him hopefully.

"That's just what I'm thinking," he says.

"Can you manage this with your crutches?" she asks, pointing to the pot holding the turkey.

He nods.

"I'll hand it to you." She deftly grabs the pot and twists back toward him; the sudden movement showers salty water on his face, which seems to wake him up. For a moment she fears he'll slip on the water accumulating on the floor, but he grabs the pan with the turkey, stabilizing his weight on his good foot, while his tongue licks the salty brine on his lips.

"I'll help," she says, rushing down.

Rudolph's at the door. "Chef wants the second turkey down," he says. As he hops onto the ladder, his warm body brushes against Elena's—and when he hands her the second turkey, his soft, strong hand lingers on hers so that they're holding the bird together. She doesn't want to move away. Their hands touch and their eyes connect deeply in a special dance. She feels a delightfully light feeling feather through her body—something like a tickle, but not the one she feels for Frank. She wonders at this energy; it's a feeling she's not had before. Amazed, she wants it to last forever. But remembering the task at hand, she takes a step backward, severing contact with Rudolph.

"I'm not going to be able to carry this out there with these crutches," Frank admits.

"I've got it," Rudolph says, swooping down from the ladder. He grabs the pot, flashing a smile at Elena, and carries the turkey out to the kitchen.

Elena follows with her turkey, with Frank hobbling behind.

"You know how to prep the birds?" Fred asks.

Elena nods and makes a space for herself at the butcher table. Maintaining her focus, she begins to carve out the first turkey's insides, removing the liver and the giblets, the neck, the heart, and the kidneys to save them for the gravy; then she rinses and pats the bird dry. She handles the bird with confidence; she could do this with her eyes closed. She moves on to the second turkey.

"I'm planning to cook one turkey intact, but the second needs to be cut into parts for individual roasting," Fred says.

"I can do that," she says, and when she's done cleaning the bird, she chooses a six-inch stainless steel knife and begins to cut it into its pieces.

The knife cuts with ease, and soon she has an audience.

"Wow," Rudolph says, sidling up to her.

"Where'd you learn to handle a boning knife like that?" Maya asks, her eyes like beacons.

"I can show you," Elena says, looking directly at Frank, who stands nearby, shaking his head proudly, like an encouraging brother to a younger sister.

Elena focuses on her work, explaining what she's learned from Baba as she cuts. She's aware all eyes are on her, watching her working on the wing: pulling it away from the body and then cutting the hollow area between the wing and the breast. She doesn't mind. They watch her in the way she watched Fred so competently treat the acorns.

Fred, a smile on his face, pulls up a seat and watches too.

"There's a wing bone," Rudolph says, assisting as she cuts through and continues to pull the wing.

When the wing releases from the body, she goes to the other side.

"Can I do it?" Rudolph asks.

She hands him the knife. He cuts the upper portion at the elbow joint and then picks up the turkey wing drumettes, jokingly putting them between his teeth. Elena laughs at his playfulness. Then she asks Fred if he wants her to separate the middle wing from the wing tip.

"Good idea—you're ahead of me, Elena," he says. "Good for soup stock."

Elena nods.

"I could use you around here as my apprentice, you know," he says.

Elena stares at him. "Really?"

Fred nods. "No kidding! I'm offering you a job."

Everyone claps, including Frank, who gives Elena a wide-eyed look.

Upon hearing Fred's offer, Maya and Rudolph and Frank all cheer and pat Elena on the back. She looks up and feels a new feeling inside she can't name. What is it? It's like when Baba screamed and raved when Elena completed an impossible task, but different—so straightforward and encouraging, even joyful, and from kids her age. She feels acceptance.

With a clarity inside about her skills coupled with the joy of others, Elena feels incredible. She celebrates her good fortune, feeling light and happy, as she continues her task, methodically cutting the legs from the body, revealing the joints as she cuts, pushing on the leg, opening the joint, and then finally cutting through it, leaving the thigh and drumstick intact.

Now she cuts along the rib cage from the tail end to the neck on each side of the bird so as to remove the breast from the body cavity. She splits the breast in half and cuts along the edge of the wishbone on the keel bone. She uses short, swiping cuts along the ribs to remove them from the breast half.

"Voilà, a boneless breast," Maya says with glee in her eyes.

Elena lowers her head as if she's bowing, full of gratitude. Fred takes the parts and returns them to a smaller fridge, and the teenagers resume their shucking and paring of vegetables—but this time they gab, saluting her skills and asking her if she wants to come to the park with them, or to eat at their houses, or go to a concert. She feels a thrill at how her wish for friends her age is suddenly coming true.

Elena feels like she's crossed a threshold from a fairy tale girl to a real teenager, sitting here in real time in Fred's restaurant, teaching her peers how to debone a turkey and receiving offers of friendship.

She is still basking in this feeling when she overhears Fred and Frank conversing.

"She's amazing!" Fred says to Frank.

"Yeah, she looks like she belongs here."

"From acorn flour to turkey deboning—I'd be a fool not to offer her a job," Fred says.

At the end of the afternoon, Elena readies herself to leave, gathering with Maya and Rudolph at the door, her red sack slung over her left shoulder and across her chest. She knows she looks different from the others in her white cape and woolen skirt and red bag, what with Maya dressed in a colorful print top over ripped jeans and Rudolph wearing a Washington High sweatshirt and pants belted low at the waist, but she feels connected to them.

"Hey Elena," Frank calls.

She turns to face him.

"I'm happy for you, sis," he says.

CHAPTER 24: *Thanksgiving Day*

Thrilled that Elena hadn't wanted a ride home after the long shift at the bistro, but instead wanted to walk into the night with Maya and Rudolph, Frank smiled. She preferred to be with other teenagers. And besides, he was delighted to hang back with Fred and marvel with him over Elena's knife skills.

When they finished up in the kitchen, they climbed into Fred's car to head home.

"Could we stop by Our Lady on the way?" Frank asked Fred as his brother pulled away from the curb. He wanted to speak with Father Al.

Fred waited in the car while Frank went inside. Approaching the vestibule, he saw the shadow of the priest through a stained glass window near the door, an elongated silhouette in long skirt and cap. Before he even knew what he was doing he was standing beside the old man, who seemed deep in contemplation, his fingers entangled in his long beard.

"Father, may I speak with you?" he asked.

Father Al turned toward him. His soft white beard, bushy eyebrows, and long hair made him look like Santa Claus. "Yes, of course."

Frank could hear his heart beating in excitement over Elena becoming part of his family. Now he wanted to get to know her guardian.

"Come with me, son," the priest said, and together they walked through the vestibule, beyond the chapel, and into a cozy kitchen space. The priest closed the door and motioned for Frank to sit at the small wooden table, poured him a cup of tea from a small carafe, and sat down across from him.

Frank wasn't sure what to do with his crutches.

Father Al, seemingly reading his lost expression, reached out for the sticks. "What happened to your foot?" he asked, rising and placing the crutches in the corner of the small room.

"An accident," Frank said. "Elena saved my life in the park on the night she was picking acorns." He took a sip of the sweet warm tea from the cup Father Al had placed in front of him.

"That part I know," Father Al said. "You were chosen to be part of the mystery, son."

Frank didn't understand what that meant, exactly, but he knew it to be true. And the priest's voice calmed him. Frank was not religious and yet recent events were like magic—like some kind of miracle. He supposed it could just as easily be spiritual, certainly mysterious.

"Chosen, you say? For what, Father?"

"Why, son, you are close now to your original nature—who you are meant to be, or should I say, who you *are*." Father Al took a sip of his tea. "You are meant to see clearly, to serve others."

Frank squinted. Puzzled by but appreciative for the priest's kind words, he bowed his head. He felt seen.

"You have been initiated into the great mystery," Father Al said.

Frank held on to his seat. He wanted to ask this wise, learned man about the mystery, about his participation in everything he'd witnessed, but he hadn't really participated through intention. His only intention had been to save Elena from harm. Perhaps that was good enough. He sat contemplating, feeling his breath move slowly through his body.

"Father, I saw the spark that set Anya aflame. I saw her dissolve."

The priest nodded and, looking like he'd just remembered something, got up, went to a nearby bookshelf, and took out a book. On its spine were the words, *A Book of Blessings*.

He came back and sat down. "I dabble in poetry. Do you write, son?"

Frank shook his head; he didn't know poetry except the poem he'd written to the salamanders.

Father Al opened the book to a well-worn page and started reading to him:

Hush, my son. Listen for the unbroken cord.
Journeys through darkness begin with an inner spark
lighting a flame of love,
breaking the spell, turning night into day.

Blessed are we who witness the dissolve of evil,
which ends an ancient curse.
For now the sun calls forth the dawn of a new day.
We are alive to see and drink this cup of joy.

Frank liked it, especially the line about the one spark being all one needs to break a spell—yet he still wasn't sure how this applied to what he'd seen.

"We want to explain our world concretely, and sometimes there is something vast and more spacious," Father Al explained. "We must turn to the poets to make room for the unknown."

"But what I witnessed doesn't happen usually. I saw them all disappear."

"Then you are blessed." The priest reached for his hand.

They sat hand in hand, facing each other, for a few moments in silence.

"Father, I'm not sure where to go from here," Frank said, feeling tenderness in his heart space.

"You will find your way. You must have faith."

Father Al stood up. He looked tired. "If you'll excuse me, I must return to my prayers," he said. "Thank you for helping Elena."

"She's helped me as well," Frank said simply. "Oh, Father, one more thing . . ." He told the priest about Elena's day at the restaurant, and Fred offering her a job. "She's an incredible worker," he said.

The priest bowed his head. "Yes, she is. Please thank your brother for giving her work, I know she will thrive there."

Father Al gestured for Frank to lead the way out. Frank hesitated.

"Is there anything else?" the priest asked.

"Will you join us at the restaurant tomorrow mid-morning to celebrate and eat acorn pancakes with us?" Frank asked, putting a card into Father Al's hand.

A glimmer in his eyes, the priest nodded. Then he bowed to Frank, and Frank felt his own eyes glistening with tears.

"We actually have freshly sifted acorn flour," Fred told his team at the bistro early the next morning. He went to the small fridge and returned with a covered bowl. Everyone gathered round as he removed the lid, revealing finely ground flour—a black mountain with a steep-looking peak, silky as a baby's skin.

"Ahh!" Rudolph said. "I've never seen such finely sifted flour! Where did you get it?"

"Our thanks to Elena," Frank said, looking at her.

"Amazing!" Maya said. "How'd you do it?" She stared at Elena. Elena blushed at the attention.

"I have the recipe for you, Maya," Fred interrupted. Didn't you do a project on the California's Native tribes?"

"Yes," she said, "the Ohlone and the Coast Miwoks."

"These are Cherokee griddlecakes," Fred said. "Not a California tribe, of course, but we'll cook them and celebrate the Ohlone and Miwoks in gratitude for the privilege of living on their land on Thanksgiving Day."

"Yes, and we have a surprise guest today," Frank announced. "Father Al will be joining us in half an hour." He looked at Elena.

"Oh! I am so happy," Elena said, raising her hands up in front of her face.

"Father Al?" Rudolph asked quietly.

"He is my beloved guardian," Elena explained, as Fred set to work mixing the flour and milk, melted butter, a taste of sugar, and eggs all together and then spooning out the batter onto the hot griddle. They watched as the butter sizzled at the edges of the griddle, creating fluted brown edges.

Rudolph set out another place setting. The dishes and silverware sparkled on a starched white linen. Mugs waited patiently to be filled with coffee or hot apple cider.

Frank nodded, smiled, and watched as Fred expertly flipped the shimmering acorn griddlecakes, which seemed to shiver with delight. When the knock on the door came, he hastened to open it. Father Al stood there holding wild boysenberry jam and freshly whipped butter.

Elena rushed up to greet him. "I'm so happy you came today, Father Al! Come, come meet my friends, Maya and Rudolph. And Fred. You know Frank."

Father Al looked at each one and bowed gently. "I stopped at the Cinderella Bakery," he said, offering the jam to Fred.

"Welcome, Father Al—we're so happy to meet you," Fred said, taking the proffered jam.

"Let's break bread together," Rudolph said, eyeing the sizzling pancakes on the griddle.

"But first, Father, will you lead us in a Thanksgiving prayer?" Frank asked. "Maybe the poem you read for me last night?" He thought about his own first poem, "Ode to a Salamander," and felt a yearning to read and write more poetry. He was on his way to growing his arms and legs and new lungs to breathe in the world.

"Of course, my son," said Father Al, and for the second time in twelve hours, Frank listened intently to the blessing: "Listen to the unbroken cord."

CHAPTER 25:

The Fulfillment of Dreams

*I*n her attic room, Elena thinks about her new friends and remembers how she dreamed about having a sister when she was growing up. Elena wants nothing more than to spend time with Maya and to be part of her friend group. Maya has invited her to her graduation from Washington High in June, and Elena's ecstatic. She feels she has reunited with Vasilisa—only Maya is alive and others can see her too.

When Elena meets Maya's family a few days later, she knows her life is expanding and her childhood dream has come true.

With Rudolph, Elena climbs trees in Oak Glen, sits side by side with him up in the canopy of the largest oak, and watches the moon rise. In the coming year he will attend Berkeley and tell her his stories of being a student there, "dorming" with other kids his age, and talk about his summer plans for an archaeological dig. Holding her hand, Rudolph will invite her to join him in Teotihuacan, forty miles northeast of Mexico City—the largest city of the Pre-Columbian Americas—for his research project.

Father Al will pay Elena's fare and she'll see the dig as a path to reconnect her with the ancestors and the ancestral earth. She'll piece together the backbones of an ancient people. The bones will help her reimagine the hidden life carried in the earth, and help her imagine into the future, too. She knows excavating with Rudolph at the ancient sites will bring her closer to the continuity of human-kind. Not only will she tenderly brush clean the bones of ancient ones, a task familiar and comforting, but she will be doing it with Rudolph. Roaming in the desert between the Temple of the Sun and the Temple of the Moon, they will feel the heat and the dust on their skin with the big sky overhead. They will tunnel through the secret inner passages underground and in their own bodies. After the work is done, they will lie on the pyramids at night under the stars.

When it's time to leave Mexico, they'll step from their perch under the sky canopy, follow the stars along the handle of the Big Dipper, and, as always, hold each other tenderly.

Back at home in San Francisco, Elena will continue working at the bistro. On Sundays, Father Al will eat with them at the restaurant and together they'll write their silly letters to Frank—a handwritten line from each of them, in turn, over and over, until the page is full. Father Al will mail them to him in Myanmar every Monday morning.

At the end of her second year working with him at the restaurant, Fred will gift Elena a year at Le Cordon Bleu.

In time, Elena will have a child with Rudolph. Their child, Christina, will play with her puppy on the bunk with a hay palette for a mattress in the familiar rustic house on Taraval, remodeled just enough so as to make it more comfortable for their little family; they will be careful not to disturb its earthy essence. Elena will sing her daughter "Kalinka," the song Father Al sang to her, and read her the fairy tale "Vasilisa the Beautiful," and one day while they dance and sing, Kukla will find her way into Christina's dress pocket.

One day not so long after, Christina will poke her tiny finger into an opening in the doll's soft body and pull out thin strands of hair woven into braids and attached to a tiny silver heart. When she opens the locket, she'll find a picture—a baby and a mama. The baby looks just like her mama. She'll run to her daddy, crying, "Daddy, Daddy, Daddy, look! A picture of Mommy and a lady. Mommy looks just like me!"

Seeing the doll and the locket will invite Elena's memory of Baba Vera and De-doo Victor, who gave her impossible tasks that led her to freedom. They brought her to the glen to save Frank's life; to the baths to kill the wicked witch Anya; to the bistro to become a fine chef; to Rudolph and the excavation fields; to the birth of physical love and a child.

Kukla, though no longer a physical touchstone for Elena, will stay near her and reside inside her heart as a guiding light. Elena will comfort her daughter in the way Kukla always comforted her, by encouraging her intuition.

One day, when Elena hears her guests arriving for their weekly Sunday visit, she will peek from the window of the old studio where Victor used to work and find, to her surprise, that Frank is standing outside. He will be wearing a long burgundy robe—earned in the temples of Myanmar, where he will have spent many years—and he will open the passenger door of his yellow cab for Father Al. Henry O will be there, and Fred will be sitting in the backseat, holding a bouquet of wild roses.

As in a fairy tale, they'll live happily ever after.

EPILOGUE:

Vasilisa the Beautiful and Baba Yaga

*I*n a certain realm there once lived a merchant. Although he had been married for twelve years, he had only one daughter, Vasilisa the Beautiful.

When the maid was eight years old, her mother fell ill. As she lay dying, the merchant's wife called her little daughter to her, took a doll from under the coverlet, and said, "Listen, dear Vasilisa. Remember and heed my last words. I leave you this little doll with my blessing. Keep it with you always and do not show it to a soul. If you are ever in trouble, give the doll something to eat and ask its advice. It will take your food and tell you what to do."

With that, the mother kissed the child and died.

The merchant remarried a woman with two daughters. Autumn came, and he left to sell his wares . . .

"There's no light in the house and our work is not done," said one of Vasilisa's stepsisters one evening. "Someone must run to Baba Yaga's for a light."

"You will have to go," both stepsisters shouted to Vasilisa. "Off you go to Baba Yaga!" And they pushed Vasilisa out of the room.

The poor little girl went to her garret and pulled out her doll. "Come, little doll, eat up your supper while I pour my troubles into your ear."

"Never fear, Vasilisa," it said, "do as they say, but keep me with you all the time. As long as I am with you, Baba Yaga can do you no harm."

Vasilisa got ready, put the doll in her pocket, and, crossing herself, went off into the dense forest.

Vasilisa walked through night and day, and only the next day did she come to the glade where Baba Yaga's hut stood. The fence around the hut was made of human bones, and on each stake was a human skull with glaring eyes.

Vasilisa stood rooted to the spot, trembling with fear.

Soon a terrible noise rushed through the forest: The trees creaked, the dry leaves crackled, and out of the forest came Baba Yaga, riding in a mortar, driving herself along with a pestle. . . . "Fee, fo! I smell the blood of a Russian! Who is there?"

"It is I, Grannie," Vasilisa said. "Stepmother's daughters sent me for a light."

"Very well," said Baba Yaga. "I know them. You must stay here and work for me, then I'll give you a light. If not, I'll eat you up!"

When the sun rose, Baba Yaga gave Vasilisa an impossible number of tasks to do, then got into her mortar and off she went, driving herself along with the pestle and sweeping her traces away with a besom.

Vasilisa was now alone. She looked around the witch's hut, amazed at such abundance, and then wondered which of her many chores she should start first. She began to despair; how would she ever finish them all before evening?

But lo and behold—all her work was done! And there was the little doll, separating the last husks from the wheat.

"Oh, my rescuer," Vasilisa said to her little doll, "you have saved me from a cruel fate."

"All you have to do now," said the doll, slipping back into Vasilisa's pocket, "is cook the dinner. Cook it with God's help, the rest to your heart's content."

Toward evening Vasilisa, laid the table and sat waiting for Baba Yaga. As it grew dark, the black horseman flashed by the gate and night fell. Only the skulls' eyes were gleaming.

The trees began to creak, the leaves to crackle; Baba Yaga was on her way. When Vasilisa met her at the door, she shouted, "Is it all done?"

"Pray, see for yourself, Grannie," said Vasilisa.

Baba Yaga took a good look. Annoyed that there was nothing to complain about, she said, "Very well."

The next morning, Baba Yaga went off again in her mortar, leaving Vasilisa with yet another mountain of tasks to complete, including picking poppy seeds from a pile of what seemed like thousands of flowers.

Vasilisa and her doll soon had the work done. When the old witch returned, she took a good look and cried, "My loyal servants, my faithful friends, press oil from the poppy seeds!"

Three pairs of hands appeared, took the poppy seeds, and carried them out of sight. Then Baba Yaga sat down to eat.

Vasilisa stood by in silence

"Why don't you say something?" asked Baba Yaga. "Haven't you got a tongue in your head?"

"I do not dare to speak unless you allow it," answered Vasilisa, "but by your leave, I wish to ask you a question."

"Go on," the old hag said, "but not every question brings good: Those who know too much grow old too soon."

"I only want to ask you about what I have seen, Grannie. As I was coming here, a horseman on a white steed rode by, all white himself and dressed in white; whoever can he be?"

"He is my day so light," said Baba Yaga.

"Then a second horseman overtook me riding a red horse, all red himself and dressed in red; who is he?"

"He is my sun so bright," said Baba Yaga.

"And a black horseman who overtook me right by your gate, Grannie?"

"He is my darkest night. All of them are my loyal servants."

Vasilisa at once recalled the three pairs of hands and fell silent.

"Why don't you ask more questions?" asked Baba Yaga.

"Let that be all," the girl replied. "You said yourself that those who know too much grow old too soon, Grannie."

"It's good you ask only about what you saw outside, not inside. I don't like gossips in my house; I eat folks who are too inquisitive. Now I have a question for you: How do you manage to do all the work I set you?"

"My mother's blessing helps me," answered Vasilisa.

"So that's it! Then get you gone, blessed daughter! I want no blessed ones here." With that she quickly dragged Vasilisa out of the hut, pushed her through the gates, took a skull with burning eyes from the fence, stuck it on a stick, and gave it to her, saying, "Here is a light for your stepsisters. Take it; that is what they sent you here for."

Vasilisa ran home by the light of the skull, which did not go out until daybreak; finally, by nightfall next evening, she reached home.

She looked up at her stepmother's house and, seeing no light in the window, decided to enter with the skull.

For the first time since her mother's death, she was welcomed kindly at home. Her stepsisters told her that ever since she had gone, there had been no light in the house.

"Perhaps your fire will last," her stepmother said.

The skull burned brightly inside the house, but it kept staring at Vasilisa's stepmother and stepsisters. No matter where they tried to hide, the eyes followed them.

By morning, they were all burnt to cinders. Only Vasilisa remained unharmed.

Vasilisa buried the skull in the ground, locked and bolted the house, went off to town, and asked a lonely old woman to take her in. And there she lived, waiting for her father's return. To earn her keep, Vasilisa asked the old woman to buy the best flax, and she would weave linens for her to sell.

She asked her little doll for help.

"Bring me an old comb, an old shuttle, and a horse's mane, and I'll fashion a loom for you," the doll said.

Vasilisa gathered all that was required and went to bed; during the night, the little doll made a splendid loom. Vasilisa set to work. She spun quickly and well, and the thread came out as fine and smooth as the hair on her head.

By winter's end, the linen was all woven. Vasilisa presented it to the old woman.

"Granny," she said, "go and sell this linen and keep the money for yourself."

The old woman looked at the linen with wide eyes. "No, dear child! Such linen may be worn by no one but the king. I'll take it to the palace."

So the old woman took the shirts to the king. In the meantime, Vasilisa washed her face, combed her hair, dressed, and sat by the window, waiting to see what would come to pass.

Before long, a servant of the king came into the yard. He entered the room and said, "The king wishes to see the seamstress who made the fine linen for his shirts. He wishes to reward her with his own royal hands."

So off went Vasilisa to appear before the king.

No sooner did the king set eyes upon Vasilisa than he fell in love with her. "I cannot part with you, my fair maiden," he said. "You will be my wife."

Taking Vasilisa by her lily-white hands, he sat her down beside him, and the wedding was held without ado.

Shortly afterward, Vasilisa's father returned. He was overjoyed by her good fortune. Both he and the old woman went to live in the palace with Vasilisa and the king.

And, of course, she carried her little doll in her pocket always, till the end of her days.

Acknowledgments

Without Brooke Warner, my writing coach and mentor, there would be no Frances Pia, no Lavinia Lavinia, and now Elena. Thank you Krissa Lagos for the exceptional copy edit, keeping me straight on verb tenses and more. Thank you, Shannon Green, my project manager at She Writes Press (SWP), for always being available.

This modern-day fairy tale, where other worldly beings meet up with a San Francisco cabdriver, was inspired by a Russian fairy tale, "Vasilisa the Beautiful and Baba Yaga," which I first read in Clarissa Pinkola Estés's *Women Who Run with the Wolves: Myths and Stories of the Wild Woman Archetype*.

As a psychologist I have spent many hours reading and listening to Dr. Clarissa Pinkola Estés, whose writing and oral stories have greatly influenced *The Girl in the White Cape*. When I first read the Russian fairy tale, I was enamored with the story of the doll and its relation to feminine intuition as Dr. Estés delineates. It made sense that we must nurture our intuition and hold it dearly in our pockets. When an opportunity came in 2002 to consult with Russian colleagues in St. Petersburg, I arranged a role-playing with our consultation group, each member playing a different character in the fairy tale. They knew it, of course. It was incredible to see the various parts of ourselves come together in that room.

When I returned to San Francisco I started thinking about writing a modern-day version of the story. I envisioned a young girl of fifteen in a white cape, living with a Baba Yaga named Vera on Taraval Street in San Francisco. In my novel Elena lives in a fairy-tale dream and finds her intuition with the help of the doll pinned to her nightie. Father Al, her Russian priest guardian, and Baba Vera, a wacky witch, support her when an ugly witch stepmother arrives in a taxi from the San Francisco Airport with Frank, a twenty-five-year-old cab driver whose naïve and porous qualities become intertwined with her fate.

As I finish this novel, I immediately feel my gratitude for Dr. Estés's influence on my imagination for stories. Thrilled and grateful for her encouragement to me and others to trust our own feminine intuition as a guide in difficult and not so difficult times.

Thank you, Alexander Afanasyev, for compiling old folklore such as Vasilisa the Wise, Vasilisa the Beautiful and Baba Yaga, Vasilisa the Fair with similar themes of good and evil, and trust.

Thank you to my spiritual teachers: Mark Coleman, Jaune Evans, Frank Ostaseski, Jack Kornfield, and Spirit Rock Meditation Center in Woodacre, and now deceased Sister Mary Neill, Spiritual Director, Dominican College—you are my dream being.

Thank you dear readers, Kathy Andrew, Janet Constantino, Gay Galleher, Sue Salenger, Susan Shaddick, Marsha Trent, Marlene Douglas, Ken Wilk, and Peter Sapienza.

Thanks to recent writing teachers Nadine Kenney Johnstone, Andrea Firth, Janine de Boisblanc; Fromm writing teachers Lynne Kaufman, Lily Iona MacKenzie, Joan Minninger, Cary Pepper; and the Fromm Players from whom I continue to learn.

Thank you to my friends. I love you.

Last but not least my dear family—Peter my husband for fifty-seven years. Wow Peter! Thank you Peter and Elisa Sapienza, my son and daughter; Milla Sapienza and Isabella Farfan, my granddaughters, who bring magic to me and to whom I dedicate this novel.

About the Author

*B*arbara Sapienza, PhD, is a retired clinical psychologist and an alumna of San Francisco State University's creative writing master's program. She writes and paints, nourished by her spiritual practices of meditation, tai chi, and dance. Her family, friends, and grandchildren are her teachers. Her first novel, *Anchor Out* (She Writes Press, 2017), received an IPPY Bronze for Best Regional Fiction, West Coast. Her second novel, *The Laundress* (She Writes Press, 2020), received a starred review from *Kirkus Reviews*. Sapienza lives in Sausalito, California, with her husband.

Author photo © Chris Loomis

SELECTED TITLES FROM SHE WRITES PRESS

She Writes Press is an independent publishing
company founded to serve women writers everywhere.
Visit us at www.shewritespress.com.

The Laundress by Barbara Sapienza. $16.95, 978-1-63152-679-4.
Lavinia Lavinia is haunted by the secret of why was she whisked
away from Italy and brought to San Francisco at four years old by
her uncle, and what happened to her parents. Through the sacred
ritual of washing clothes, she unfolds memories and a new family,
unraveling her own heritage and sense of self.

Clara at the Edge by Maryl Jo Fox. $16.95, 978-1-63152-250-5.
Seventy-three-year-old Clara, a stubborn widow, must finally
reconcile with her estranged son and face the guilty secrets tied
to her daughter's death—with the help of a rowdy spirit guide in
the form of a magic purple wasp.

Size Matters by Cathryn Novak. $16.95, 978-1-63152-103-4. If you
take one very large, reclusive, and eccentric man who lives to eat,
add one young woman fresh out of culinary school who lives to
cook, and then stir in a love of musical comedy and fresh-brewed
exotic tea, with just a hint of magic, will the result be a soufflé—or
a charred, inedible mess?

South of Everything by Audrey Taylor Gonzalez. $16.95, 978-1-63152-949-8. A powerful parable about the changing South after World War II, told through the eyes of young white woman whose friendship with her parents' black servant, Old Thomas, initiates her into a world of magic and spiritual richness.

The Trouble With Becoming A Witch by Amy Edwards. $16.95, 978-1-63152-405-9. Veronica thinks she's happy. But with fight after fight, night after night, she knows that something isn't right anymore. Then her husband busts her researching witchcraft—and her picturesque suburban life is turned upside down.

Bridge of the Gods by Diane Rios. $16.95, 978-1-63152-244-4. When twelve year-old Chloe Ashton is abducted and sold to vagabonds, she is taken deep into the Oregon woods, where she learns that the old legends are true: animals can talk, mountains do think, and deep in the forests, the trees still practice their old ways.